W9-CIA-734

"I Think It's A Rule—No Birthday Should Pass Without A Birthday Kiss."

He was teasing, she thought. Only, in the next second, he buried his long, strong fingers in her curls, holding her head tilted up to his.

His lips touched hers, softer than honey. He was just teasing, she mentally repeated to herself. A neighborly kiss. A gesture of affection. If she just stood still for a second, it'd be over.

But for some strange reason, he seemed in no hurry.

No one had ever kissed her like this. He hadn't even touched her body, yet every nerve ending in her body seemed electrified. Yearning swept through her like a storm, so heady and wild that her knees wanted to buckle. She felt young and reckless. She felt brand-new, back in that time when she really believed in fairy tales and in the unconquerable power of love....

Dear Reader,

Welcome to a wonderful new year at Silhouette Desire! Let's start with a delightfully humorous MAN OF THE MONTH by Lass Small—*The Coffeepot Inn*. Here, a sinfully sexy hero is tempted by a virtuous woman. He's determined to protect her from becoming the prey of the local men—*and* he's determined to win her for himself!

The HOLIDAY HONEYMOONS miniseries continues this month with *Resolved To (Re)Marry* by Carole Buck. Don't miss this latest installment of this delightful continuity series!

And the always wonderful Jennifer Greene continues her STANFORD SISTERS series with *Bachelor Mom*. As many of you know, Jennifer is an award winner, and this book shows why she is so popular with readers and critics alike!

Completing the month are a new love story from the sizzling pen of Beverly Barton, *The Tender Trap;* a delightful Western from Pamela Macaluso, *The Loneliest Cowboy;* and something a little bit different from Ashley Summers, *On Wings of Love*.

Enjoy!

Lucia Macro

Senior Editor

Please address questions and book requests to:
Silhouette Reader Service
U.S.: 3010 Walden Ave., P.O. Box 1325, Buffalo, NY 14269
Canadian: P.O. Box 609, Fort Erie, Ont. L2A 5X3

JENNIFER GREENE
BACHELOR MOM

Eau Claire District Library

SILHOUETTE *Desire*
Published by Silhouette Books
America's Publisher of Contemporary Romance

109380

If you purchased this book without a cover you should be aware
that this book is stolen property. It was reported as "unsold and
destroyed" to the publisher, and neither the author nor the
publisher has received any payment for this "stripped book."

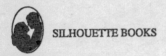 SILHOUETTE BOOKS

ISBN 0-373-76046-9

BACHELOR MOM

Copyright © 1997 by Jennifer Greene

All rights reserved. Except for use in any review, the reproduction
or utilization of this work in whole or in part in any form by any
electronic, mechanical or other means, now known or hereafter
invented, including xerography, photocopying and recording, or in
any information storage or retrieval system, is forbidden without
the written permission of the editorial office, Silhouette Books,
300 East 42nd Street, New York, NY 10017 U.S.A.

All characters in this book have no existence outside the imagination of
the author and have no relation whatsoever to anyone bearing the same
name or names. They are not even distantly inspired by any individual
known or unknown to the author, and all incidents are pure invention.

This edition published by arrangement with Harlequin Books S.A.

® and TM are trademarks of Harlequin Books S.A., used under license.
Trademarks indicated with ® are registered in the United States Patent
and Trademark Office, the Canadian Trade Marks Office and in other
countries.

Printed in U.S.A.

JENNIFER GREENE

lives near Lake Michigan with her husband and two children. Before writing full-time, she worked as a teacher and a personnel manager. Michigan State University honored her as an "outstanding woman graduate" for her work with women on campus.

Ms. Greene has written more that forty category romances, for which she has won numerous awards, including the RITA for Best Short Contemporary Book, and both a Best Series Author and a Lifetime Achievement Award from *Romantic Times*.

One

Gwen Stanford didn't drink. Sobriety was no cause with her. She had nothing against alcohol; she just never had time to take up the vice—or any other vices, for that matter.

Tonight it was going to be a real different story.

Standing on her kitchen counter, she groped blindly at the back of her tallest cupboard for the shape of the rum bottle. It had to be there. Every Christmas she made the traditional family recipe for rum cake. Personally, she hated the taste of that rum cake with a passion, but her sisters loved it, and tradition was tradition. More to the immediate point, though, that bottle represented her entire liquor supply. It was rum or nothing.

There. Her fingers connected with the shape of the dusty bottle. She hooked her hand around it, risked her life leaping down from the counter, then filched a *Lion King* water glass from the shelf.

Clean dishes were waiting to be emptied from the dishwasher. Bills needed to be opened and paid. Her sons had scattered schoolbooks and toys, and the kitchen table still had some uncleaned-up crumbs. The wash was calling to her from the laundry room, and with two half-pint-size boys, letting wash pile up was begging for disaster.

Still, when a woman was determined to be wicked, no chore was too huge to be ignored.

Filled with resolve, she carried her drinking supplies and a small wrapped package, tied with a red bow, through the Florida room and out the glass doors. The package was a birthday present from her youngest sister, Paige, but so far she hadn't had a second free all day to open it. She could barely catch a free moment to breathe—but that was about to change.

Outside, the sun had just dropped below the horizon, and the sky was painted with dusky blues and scarlets. Typical of St. Augustine in September, the night was warm, redolent with the mixed smells of tangy ocean air and late-blooming flowers. House lights were popping on all over the neighborhood, but her backyard was as quiet as peace.

Exactly what she wanted. Barefoot, she flopped in the chaise longue on the patio, poured a wallop of a drink and slugged down a sip. It burned like liquid smoke all the way down her throat and tasted worse than cough syrup. Stubbornly she gulped down another couple of slugs. Maybe it was extremely doubtful that rum was ever going to be her vice of choice, but she was determined to give it a lion's try.

She reached for Paige's present and pulled at the red bow, trying to fathom the strange, unsettling dissatisfaction that had hounded her like a shadow all day. She'd been as restless as a wet cat, and had the stupidest inclination to cry. She'd never been restless, and the whole world knew that Gwen Stanford was no whiner or crier.

Nothing had even gone wrong. Josh and Jacob, thank heavens, were tucked in bed and sleeping harder than tired puppies. Jacob's first day in school had been a landmark, but the rest of the day had been pretty status quo. She'd carpooled, done accounting all morning, somehow got talked into mothering a den of Cub Scouts, made cookies for the church bake sale, shopped, took the kids out to dinner for her birthday and survived their sugar high after overdosing on cake and ice cream. The day started and ended at a hundred miles an hour, but that was like saying the Pope was Catholic. Hardly headline news.

As she opened the package from Paige, though, her heart stopped racing like an overheated engine. Strangely, her pulse started chugging in slow time. Real slow time. One look at the gift put a thick, heavy lump in her throat.

Days before, her oldest sister Abby had sent a dress for her birthday—ivory Chinese silk, as simple and elegant in style as it was sexy. Maybe the arrival of that dress had been the pinpoint moment in time when this pervasive, stupid moodiness had begun. She loved her sisters. The three women had always been impossibly different in nature and temperament, but they were unbeatably close. And Abby had unerringly chosen a dress that fit Gwen perfectly, a dress she loved and yearned to wear—yet doubted she ever would. A working bachelor mom with two young, rambunctious sons just had no time or occasion to dress up in silk.

The gift from Paige was equally personal and equally unsettling, but in an entirely different way.

Slowly Gwen lifted the cameo from the velvet box, tilting it this way and that in the fading sunset light. Paige was a cameo maker, so the choice of gift from her younger sister wasn't in itself a surprise, and Paige was an incredibly fine artist.

But this was beyond fine.

The cameo had been carved in two shades of coral. The woman in profile had short, cropped curly hair— actually, almost identical to Gwen's own hairstyle— and her arms were raised as if to joyfully embrace life. Turn the cameo just so in the light, though, and there appeared to be a sober-faced woman trapped in the darker shade of coral. The effect was subtle, but there appeared to be two women in the profile—one a shadow of the other.

Gwen reached blindly for the glass again and rapidly gulped another hefty slug of the warm rum. It burned her throat as hot as the last one did . . . as hot and stinging as this whole day had burned on her heart.

Her younger sister knew her. Too well. Damned well. Painfully well. The cameo was exquisite and could not have been a more personal present. At this particular moment, though, it hit her like a swift, sharp bullet.

Her entire life, she'd felt like a shadow.

This dissatisfied malaise wasn't really birthday caused, Gwen recognized. For some time, the nagging, lost feeling had been there. Sometimes she wondered exactly whose life she was living. Her life-style was more straight-laced than a saint's, with certainly no goof-off time built in. There never had been. But heaven knew, she'd never *planned* to be this good. Growing up, she'd never once aspired to be a saint. Where her two sisters had always had huge, identifiable life goals, though, Gwen had really only wanted one thing. Ron. From the day she met him in first grade, she'd fallen for him like a princess in a fairy tale.

Gwen lifted the rum glass, discovered it was empty and generously poured herself another splash. She squeezed her eyes closed, as if it would make swallowing the medicine a little easier.

Her divorce from Ron was two years old now. Ancient history. Yet his influence on her life certainly wasn't. With a flash of rum insight, she recognized morosely that she had always lived in Ron's shadow. She had become a bookkeeper, because that was a career she could pursue at home with the kids—and because it paid Ron's medical school bills. They lived in St. Augustine, because that was where Ron originally wanted to set up his medical practice. She'd never pursued dreams of her own, because Ron's career was so much more important than anything she wanted.

No one had ever twisted her arm to make those choices. All through those years, she'd never thought of herself as being a doormat. She'd thought she was being loving and supportive.

Somehow that looked different on her thirtieth birthday. Somehow—with the help of another gulp of rum—it occurred to her that she'd turned into a dependent, boring mouse. She didn't have a clue who Gwen Stanford even was anymore.

She'd been a wife, but she couldn't really remember being a woman. Of all the female roles she'd assumed—mom, wife, now ex-wife, bookkeeper, sister, daughter—she had no memory of setting a single goal that hadn't been to please or appease other people.

With two young sons—and God knew, Jacob and Josh were her life—she certainly couldn't take up a life-style dancing naked on tabletops. But it ached, like the stab of a knife, that not once in her entire life had she ever done anything reckless. . . .

"Gwen? Are you alive and awake over there?"

Gwen startled at the sudden deep voice, but then realized it was just Spence.

Her vision seemed oddly blurred, and real dusk had fallen now. The sky was no longer ruby and purple, but washed in a hushed royal blue. Even if it were pitch black, though, she would never mistake anyone else for Spence McKenna. His backyard bordered hers. They shared a fence—and two six-year-olds. His April had just endured the same landmark day in first grade, in the same class as her Jacob.

If she'd thought about it, she might have guessed he'd stop by for a few minutes to share parenting notes. She hadn't thought about it, and at the moment, seemed incapable of thinking about anything clearly. For some reason her tongue seemed thicker than molasses. It was a mighty struggle to sound normal. "I'm awake. Just buried in a few dark thoughts for a minute there. Come on over. Did April survive her first day with Mrs. Cox?"

"She did, but I don't know about me," Spence admitted. "I don't know what I was expecting with Mrs. Cox, but I thought she'd be older, wiser, warmer. Instead she looked younger than a teenager and seemed meaner than a drill sergeant. I figured I'd ask for your perspective, since your Josh survived her last year."

"Well, Josh survived her, but I have to admit not being thrilled with her, either. We've had some run-ins. I just think she's too tough for the little ones. Jacob came home announcing that school was stupid."

"So it wasn't just my April. Hell. Deserting her in the door of that classroom was tougher than chewing nails. There are parts of this single parenting business that I sure wish came with a manual."

Gwen chuckled. "I take it your angel's now safely in bed and you're headed straight for the fortitude?" Even with her blurred vision, she could see he was carrying a glass as he unlatched the fence gate and ambled toward her.

"Yeah. Full-strength iced tea." She caught a flash of white teeth when he noticed the bottle at her side. "That looks more like what the doctor ordered. Somehow I'd never have guessed you were a dark rum fan."

"I wasn't—until about an hour ago. Help yourself if you want some." Any second now, Gwen expected him to look a little less fuzzy. Not that it particularly made any difference. Even fuzzy and blurred at the edges, her neighbor was downright dazzling.

Spence sank into the webbed lawn chair across from her and stretched out his long legs. Suit and tie were typical workday attire for him, but at some point he'd jettisoned the suit jacket and tie. He was still wearing formal, navy suit pants, though, and his white shirt was opened at his sun-bronzed throat.

The first time Gwen had met him, her hormones had a heart attack. Still did. Spence was a six-foot-one-inch depth charge of virility, built lean and elegant,

Eau Claire District Library

with dark hair as thick as a mink's and chocolate brown eyes. Energy and drive seemed to seep from his pores. Lots of character and intelligence were written in the character lines on his face, but to heck with that, he had the slowest, sexiest smile on a man that she'd ever seen. He owned a marketing firm. Gwen had no trouble picturing him as an unstoppable dynamo in business—or with women.

If he'd been any less intimidating, Gwen doubted they'd ever have made friends. And they weren't precisely friends, more good neighbors and cosufferers in the single parent life. She knew little about his ex-wife, beyond that her name was May and she'd literally dropped the baby in Spence's lap and taken off on him. He'd moved here a couple years ago, motivated to find a house in a good school system and a neighborhood with kids. Chicken pox had initiated their first conversation—his April came down with it at the same time as her Josh. Spence had been beside himself and had come knocking on her door for advice.

Gwen curled up her legs, well aware that her hair was an unbrushed mop and her feet were bare. Her ex had been an overwhelming hunk—Ron had dominated every room he walked into—but Spence made her ex look like an untried boy. These days Gwen usually had the good sense to plaster herself against the nearest wallpaper anywhere near that type of intimidating man.

With Spence, that maestro intimidating factor ironically made him comfortable to be with. He'd seen her patchwork skirt and pink T-shirt before. He'd seen her looking like she'd been through a daylong train wreck before. Talking to him had always been easy, simply because she'd never suffered an ounce of nerves

Eau Claire District Library

that he could conceivably be personally interested in her. A dazzling panther was hardly likely to notice a cookie maker and a born den mother. He could be a feast for her housewife eyes without a kernel of risk. He already knew she was a mouse. There was nothing to hide, nothing to worry about.

It wasn't the first evening he'd sprawled in her lawn chair to waste a few minutes relaxing. "So...you looked lost in serious thoughts when I walked up. Were those dark thoughts all for Mrs. Cox?"

"Nope. To be honest, I was thinking about being reckless."

"Reckless, huh?" Spence's smile was lazy, easy, but there seemed a sudden flash of something in his eyes. When he saw her reaching for an empty glass, he leaned over and swiftly poured her another splash of rum. "Did I hear right from the kids that it's your birthday today?"

"Yup. Three-oh."

"Uh-oh. I just passed thirty-four a few months ago. That was bad enough, but those birthdays that end in zeros are always killers. Big soul-searching time, hmm?"

"'Fraid so. In fact, it was just occurring to me that I've made a total mess of my life." She frowned, unsure how that had just slipped out. Sharing chicken pox and carpooling dilemmas came a lot more naturally with Spence than anything seriously personal. She lifted her rum glass and then uneasily clunked it back down. Temporarily there seemed to be three full moons in the sky, two sets of swing sets in the backyard, and the expression in Spence's eyes seemed deep and caring and...intimate. Almost sexily intimate.

There seemed to be a teensy bundle of evidence mounting up that she'd passed her tolerance limit for rum—about two glasses ago.

Spence settled back in the shadows, but she could still feel his gaze on her face. "Now what's this about making a total mess of your life? The last I noticed, you had two damned terrific kids—"

"Yeah, I do. And I couldn't adore my monsters more. But they're about the only thing in my life that I've done right." For some unknown reason, her skirt had hiked up to her thighs. She leaned forward to push the material down. A terrible mistake. Even that slight movement made her head swim. The way Spence was looking at her made her blood sluice through her veins faster than a sled in the luge. She was, of course, imagining that look. For dead sure, she had fully intended to level part of that rum bottle, felt no guilt at all about it. But who'd have guessed a little liquor could addle her brain this fast and this foolishly?

"What is it you think you've done so wrong?" he asked gently.

"Everything."

"Like what?"

It was like a genie had opened the trapdoor on her tongue. A demon genie. Gwen was positive she never meant to answer, yet all this stupid nonsense bubbled out. "I make a living as a bookkeeper. It's a good living. Only I hate working with numbers and have always hated working with numbers. I come from Vermont, but I'm living in St. Augustine in a house my ex-husband built. It's a great house, and I love the whole area as far as raising kids. But I never chose that, either. He did. I can't think of one thing I ever chose to do—or be—on my own. Even in my family.

I have two fantastic sisters. The older one's a power-house in business, the younger one is an incredible artist. And then there's me. The mouse."

"Gwen," Spence said quietly, "you are not a mouse."

"Yeah, I am," she said stubbornly. The words were slurring; so were the thousand thoughts catapulting through her mind. But none of that dizziness seemed to soften the truth. "I've spent thirty years letting things happen to me. Instead of standing up for my-self, I just followed in the back of someone else's line. I can't even remember if or when I had any dreams or goals of my own. There just never seemed the time to figure them out. The best I can say is that I've aced the course in responsibility."

"You've had a mountain to handle alone, Gwen. And the last I noticed, being responsible was a hell of a fine quality."

"Maybe. But it's tedious and boring. I *feel* bor-ing." She pushed a hand through her spring-loaded curls. "Even trying to talk about this is pretty ridicu-lous. I don't have any choices right now. My kids are everything to me, so it's not like I could suddenly run off and join the circus. I don't *want* to join some silly circus, but darn it, Spence, I've never done one reck-less thing in my entire life."

Undoubtedly it was more of her runaway imagina-tion, but Spence suddenly seemed immobile, sitting there utterly still. "What kind of...reckless...are you thinking about?"

"I don't know. Just foolish stuff. I've never tasted caviar. Never danced in the moonlight. Never done anything so wantonly indulgent as having a manicure or a massage. Never taken off on a motorcycle and just ridden with the wind on my face, not giving a damn where I was going. And men. I've never once..."

"Never what?" Spence prompted the instant her voice trailed off.

But no amount of that demon, sweet rum could have dulled her brain into completing that thought aloud. It was in her heart, though, an itchy, unsettling awareness that she'd never known any other man but Ron, and they'd been childhood sweethearts. She'd never flirted, never been hunted and chased and romanced, never played with a grown man—and for damn sure, never felt a yearning that brought her to her knees. She doubted that feeling existed outside her dreams—and her dreams had been dominated by less-than-reputable fantasies lately. Embarrassing fantasies. Nothing like real life, nothing she would ever *really* do, and positively nothing she could ever voice aloud to a man—and especially never to Spence.

Clearly, rum or no rum, she needed to get her act together. She shook her head with a little nervous laugh. "Good grief, it's almost pitch-black. I didn't realize how late it was getting. It's way past time to head in. I owe you a big one, Spence. You came over for a little neighborly conversation, and instead I've been ranting on like a real fruitcake. I'm real sorry—"

"I was glad to listen. And there's nothing to be sorry about."

"Just forget everything I said, okay? A little case of the birthday doldrums seemed to get the best of me. I didn't really mean anything..." Something was wrong with the chaise longue. It didn't want to let her out of it. Then she remembered she needed to put her feet on the ground before she tried to stand up.

Spence lurched to his feet with a chuckle.

"Okay, I might as well admit it. I'm probably one of the hardest core drinkers you've ever met," she told him.

"I had the feeling you don't indulge too often."

"If you don't promise to forget I'm making such an idiot of myself, I'm gonna die. It was just one of those power-stress days. And I was feeling crabby. And it seemed like a drink would be a good way to relax." Once she managed to stand up, she added wryly, "My knees feel like noodles. Somehow I never expected to end up quite this relaxed."

"I think you're going to sleep well tonight. But before you go in..."

"Yes?" Just as she turned toward the door, she remembered the exquisite cameo gift from her sister. Carefully she scooped up the velvet box and slipped it safely in her skirt pocket.

"It *is* your birthday..."

She tilted her head, unsure what Spence was trying to say, unsure why he was suddenly so close. The patio cement was freezing on her bare feet, undoubtedly the reason a sudden shiver whispered up her spine. She was thinking that she needed to check on the boys, lock up, lay out clothes for tomorrow, just put this whole awful day behind her. She wasn't thinking about kissing. In a thousand million years, she would never have guessed Spence ever planned to kiss her.

"I think it's a rule—no birthday should pass without a birthday kiss," he murmured.

He was teasing, she thought. Any second now she'd think of an appropriate comeback. Only in the next second, his arms had reached over. Long, strong fingers buried in her curls, holding her head tilted up to his.

His lips touched hers, softer than honey. She could smell the warmth of his skin, taste the mint iced tea on his breath. His dark eyes caught the shimmering silver of the full moon. He was just teasing, she mentally repeated to herself. He just meant a neighbor's kiss. A gesture of affection. A kindness. If she just stood still for a second, it'd be over.

But for some strange reason, he seemed in no hurry.

Another shiver hummed up her spine, this one not caused by the icy patio cement on her bare feet. This particular shiver was as warm as a heat wave. Spence lifted his head after that first, brief taste of a kiss. His eyes were open for that moment, studying her, considering her. She saw the faintest smile on his lips, but it disappeared faster than the wink of an eye. And then he closed his eyes and came back for a real kiss.

Nothing burned like hot sugar. His mouth rubbed against hers slowly, evocatively, alluringly taking his time. She'd been married. She'd loved her husband. But no one had ever kissed her like this. All day, she'd been trying to figure out who Gwen Stanford really was. The question reared its painful head again, because God knew, she didn't know who she was at that moment.

He hadn't even touched her body, yet every nerve ending in her body seemed suddenly electrified. Her pulse was frantic, her nerves thrumming to intimate, wicked blues. He took her mouth like she was fiercely desired, like he couldn't wait another instant before touching her, like there were no swing sets and sandboxes and neighbors a few yards away, like there was nothing but her in his universe.

She'd never had such a foolish response to a man in her entire life. Family tradition or no family tradition, she abruptly resolved never to make rum cake again, to pour every ounce of that demon drink straight down the drain.

Still...

She knew, really knew, that her response to him was unforgivably silly. The hormones singing in her head had a reason. Too much rum. And the allure of a man who positively knew how to kiss a woman, who'd probably known millions and millions of women. She knew. Yet yearning still swept through her like a storm, so heady and wild that her knees wanted to buckle. She felt young and reckless. She felt brand-new, on the brink of all the excitement in life, back in that time when she really believed in fairy tales and the unconquerable power of love....

Slowly Spence stepped back from her. Slowly he traced the line of her jaw with the edge of his thumb. "Happy birthday, Gwen," he murmured.

Two

An hour later, Gwen had locked up, picked up and switched off all the lights. She dialed the telephone in her bedroom to call Vermont. Her sister should still be up, and she wanted to thank Paige for the cameo.

As the telephone rang at the other end, her gaze pounced from the lemon yellow print comforter to the wicker love seat in the corner. She'd redecorated the bedroom right after the divorce. Ron favored dark, rich expensive woods. Actually, his taste pretty predictably ran to anything that cost the moon. She'd sold the oppressive stuff, painted and redid everything in sunny yellows and white wicker. It was her private haven now. Walking into her bedroom was like walking into her own sanctuary.

Not tonight. Listening to the phone ring, she squeezed her eyes closed. If her sister wasn't home, heaven knew what she was going to do—maybe take a marathon jog around St. Augustine. She was not only feeling climb-the-walls wide awake, but sober as a judge.

That kiss from Spence could sober anyone up... although she was trying her her damnedest to work up a good case of denial. Surely it never really happened. Surely it was her imagination that he'd knocked her knickers off with that kiss. Surely it was her rum-clouded memory that made her think she'd responded to him like a wild cat.

She couldn't conceivably have responded to Spence with abandon. He was her neighbor. A *good* neighbor. He was also an experienced, sophisticated hunk. She was tuna noodle casserole and he was lobster. There was nothing wrong with being tuna noodle casserole, but man, to have him think she was sexually attracted to him was beyond mortifying. She'd never doubted that Spence ran across his share of female movers and shakers in his business life. He was probably dying of embarrassment that she'd responded to him like... well, like some sad stereotype of a sex-starved divorcee.

She hoped he'd forget it.

If he couldn't forget it, she hoped she'd explained enough times about her inexperience with rum.

Actually, she desperately hoped that if she just kept mentally denying it, maybe she could convince herself it never happened.

"Gwen! I tried to call you earlier, but you were out—I hope partying big-time. How'd the big three-oh birthday go?"

There. Her sister finally answered, and Paige's familiar alto soothed her nerves like balm for a sore. "The day's been fine, and oh, Paige, the cameo is just breathtaking. I couldn't love it more. Thank you so much!''

Paige let out a breathy sigh. "Whew. So glad you liked it. I wanted it right . . . not just some pretty piece of artwork, but something personal between you and me."

Sitting Indian-style on the bed, the phone cupped to her ear, Gwen touched the cameo pendant with soft fingers. "It was personal. More than personal. The look of the woman in the profile almost gave me the shivers . . . she almost seemed to look like me."

"I thought so, too. But I've told you before how sculpting works—any similarity like that is accidental. There's a kind of truth in any piece of raw material. The artist's job is to carve away what isn't the truth, but she can't build in a picture that isn't there. I had no way to know ahead of time that the woman was going to end up looking like you." Paige hesitated, then added deliberately, "But I wanted her to be beautiful. You're beautiful, sis. And you seem to be the only one in the entire world who isn't aware of it."

"Talk about bias." Gwen's voice was purposefully light. Maybe her sister never saw what she did. It was the shadow woman in the cameo that put a lump in her throat, not the beautiful lady who was so exuberantly embracing life. Carefully she snapped the lid closed on the velvet box. "I'll be beautiful the same day cats fly. You've just got blinders on because you're my sister."

"Hey, you're talking to the brat who put shaving cream in your bra. Short-sheeted your bed. Froze all your underpants next to Mom's jam in the freezer. Sisters don't *have* to do or say nice things."

Gwen chuckled. "Come to think of it, I'd forgotten what a brat you were. *Abby* was the nice sister."

"And what'd Abby send you for your birthday?"

"A silk dress. Ivory. Kind of swirly and soft and sexy." Maybe it was studying that cameo that made her suddenly feel restless and uneasy again, but she bounced off the bed and started pacing the room with the phone cradled against her ear. "Maybe in the year 2010, I'll find a place to wear it."

"Abby keeps trying to reform my taste in clothes, too. She should know by now it's hopeless. And how come she got all the good taste in the family?"

"I dunno. You want to short-sheet her bed the next time we see her?"

They both chuckled and wasted a few minutes creating diabolical plans for Abby and recalling all the sick practical jokes they'd pulled on each other as kids. Then Paige filled in her own family news—she'd never felt healthier in her whole life, but her new husband Stefan was miserable, suffering morning sickness big-time. As Paige embellished the details, both sisters' chuckles spilled into laughter...until Paige suddenly paused and turned serious. "Boy, I haven't heard a good belly laugh from you in forever, kiddo. I've really worried how you were doing these past few months. And you haven't said one word about the bastard."

"I wish you wouldn't call him that. He's really not, Paige. Ron's a good dad to the boys. And he didn't suddenly turn into a creep just because the marriage failed."

"I think we've had this exact same conversation before—you know I have a different opinion on that— but okay, okay. I'll try to remember not to call him a manipulative, arrogant son of a seadog in your presence, sweets. But I wish you'd try to believe it. He's well out of your life. You seeing anyone?"

"You have to be kidding. I'm not sure I've even caught sight of an adult man in six months, between being chained to the computer most of the day and den-mothering a passel of boys in my free time," Gwen said wryly. From nowhere, though, a mental picture of Spence suddenly embedded itself in her mind as if glued there.

"You've got to quit hiding in that house."

"This is my youngest sister talking? The one who hid in the art studio for years and was never going to get married as long as she lived?"

"That was before I met Stefan. Now I know what I was missing. And you, too. Just listen to me—now that I know everything," Paige teased, but again, her voice turned serious. "I know it's got to be scary to get your feet wet in the dating pool again, but everyone isn't like Ron, sis. You just have to steer clear of those high-powered, steamroller types."

"I know, I know. Believe me." Again, Spence's face flashed in her brain. He was ten times more dynamite than Ron had ever been, a clear study of a man motivated by drive and ambition and overloaded with dynamic, virile male energy. *Lord, how could she have kissed him like that?* Being a concentrated dynamo was no crime, but for her, Spence might as well have a Danger sign tattooed on his forehead. Abruptly, though, that whole thought train disappeared from her mind. "Oops...Paige, I have to go. A pint-size interruption just showed up in the doorway."

Paige chuckled just before hanging up. "Give my favorite hellion nephews a giant hug from Aunt Paige, okay?"

As it happened, only one of her hellions was standing in the door. Jacob. Tousled and barefoot and wearing his favorite cartoon pj's. He was the spitting image of his dad with his white-blond hair and woman-killer blue eyes and beyond-adorable grin. "He's back, Mom," Jacob said.

Gwen heard the quaver in his voice, and there was sure no grin on his face now. Jacob could manage to get dirty in a bathtub; he had more energy than an entire football team, and there were times he could test her patience like nobody's business. But not when he was scared. Never when he was scared.

Swiftly she reached out her arms. "Shoot. Don't tell me that blasted monster showed up again?"

"Yup. The green one. With the big bulging eyes and the claws like scissors."

"Darn. I thought we got rid of him permanently the last time."

"Nope." Another quaver, as he shot across the room and burrowed his face into her stomach. "I just came in to protect you. I wasn't scared or anything, but you're a girl and all. I figured I better sleep with you."

"Well, when one of us is afraid, I think it's a good idea to protect each other," Gwen said gravely. "But let's take care of this monster together first, okay?"

She took his hand and together they walked down the hall to his room. "Where'd he come from this time?"

"The bathroom. And then he slinked in. And then he hid by the desk."

"Ah." She switched on the big overhead light and then slowly took her time, studiously searching around the desk, bending down to look under the bed, then poking in the corners of the closet. "You see anything?" she asked her son.

"Nope."

"Any other place you think he could be hiding?"

"Aw, Mom. You don't have to keep doing this. I know it's just a dream. It's just such a *real* dream that I can't always make it go away."

"Honest, I understand. When I was six, I had pink and orange alligators under my bed. Just for the record, though... they all went away by the time I was seven. Never came back."

"Boy, were you silly. Everybody knows that alligators don't come in orange."

She made him giggle, but he still wasn't sure about leaving her alone—"unprotected"—so she curled up on the twin bed with him. It didn't take long for him to fall asleep, never did. But he didn't let her cuddle him too often, now that he was a big grown-up six-year-old, and it felt good, the warm body, the scent of her son, the cowlick tufts of his blond hair tickling her chin.

This was her life, she thought. Loving her kids. Being there for them when the monsters came.

She simply had to shake this strange, lost, dissatisfied feeling that had haunted her lately. And she simply had to put that wild, dangerous kiss from Spence out of her mind.

Before she fell asleep, she hoped fiercely that he'd just done her a kindness and forgotten all about it.

"Maybe I should sleep with you tonight."

"You think so?" Spence bent down to kiss the blue-eyed blond beauty. The love of his life had the long eyelashes of a seductress and the cajoling ways of a Lorelei. He knew—and she knew even better—that he could be had. He'd been suckered by a single milk-breath kiss before.

"There aren't any monsters in your bed, Dad. And just in case one comes, then I won't have to walk all the way down the hall to your room. It's dark and scary in the hall."

He gave April another kiss and then tucked the stuffed two-foot-high yellow rabbit under the covers with her. "There's a night light in the hall now, remember? It's not dark anymore. And I'm pretty sure we killed off all the monsters a couple nights ago. Haven't seen one since."

"But what if one comes?"

"Then you yell at the top of your lungs for Dad." He illustrated, mimicking her child's soprano in such a campy fashion that she started giggling. "I'll come running lickety-split and we'll save each other. But right now I want you to close your eyes and think about marshmallows."

"Marshmallows?"

"Yup. Close your eyes, lovebug, and concentrate real, real hard on marshmallows." It was the newest theory he was trying. So far he hadn't found a sure cure for night terrors, no matter how many child-rearing books he'd read. Instead of picturing mon-

sters just before she went to sleep, he was trying to get
her to think about something safe and soft and fun.

So far, it worked some of the time. The chances
were about "even-steven" he'd wake up in the morning with a six-year-old hogging the covers. Early in the
night, though, April's sleep patterns were as predictable as the sunrise. If he could just get her to close her
eyes, she'd be snoozing deep and heavy twenty minutes from now.

For the next twenty minutes he stood in the kitchen,
sipping an iced tea, staring out the west window at the
sweep of lawn that bordered his place and Gwen's.

Mary Margaret, his housekeeper, made fine iced
tea. She was addicted to Pine Sol, though. Seemed
there was no limit to the gallons she could go through,
and the smell pervaded the kitchen. So did the chicken
cacciatore she'd made for dinner. Mary Margaret was
chunky, built like a barrel, with long, wiry gray hair
always pulled back in the same merciless bun. She
broke something once a week, covered up any experimental cooking with an overdose of cayenne, and she
looked tougher than old nails...but she'd about die
for his daughter. Spence never cared about the rest.

He'd been a little uneasy about dads and daughters
and whether it was okay for April to climb in bed with
him in the middle of the night. Mary Margaret, in
typical tactful fashion, told him he was being stupid.
When a child was scared, you did whatever you had to
do to help them get unscared. She also told him to
burn all the silly child-rearing books and listen to her.
She'd raised five children. She knew everything.

Should he ever fail to obey her sage advice, the
threat of habanero-and-cayenne-laced chicken cacciatore was always there.

The only terrorizing females he'd allowed in his life in several years now were April and Mary Margaret.

But he was considering adding another.

Across the yard, past the shadow-dipped fence and moonlit swing set, a light went out in one of the back rooms. Gwen was putting her sons to bed. Like him, she probably couldn't really rest and relax for a few minutes yet, not until she knew for sure the kids were asleep.

Light glowed from the jalousie window in her bathroom, then flicked off again. After that she headed for the kitchen. Living across the way from her for the past two years, he knew her patterns fairly well by now. She flew around the kitchen doing little cleanups right after the boys went to bed. A few minutes later she'd check on them. She didn't let down her hair—so to speak—until she was sure her sons were asleep. Then, often enough, she'd slip off her shoes and wander outside barefoot for a few minutes, closing her eyes, breathing in the night.

It was her way of letting out the day's stresses, Spence guessed. But he'd seen her lift her face, seen the moonlight wash over her delicate profile and soft skin. Sometimes a night breeze would pucker off the ocean, cupping the blouse fabric intimately to her high, full breasts, fingering light and shine into her cap of nutmeg brown curls. Sometimes she'd sway in the breeze as if she were hearing music, not dancing, but as if there were a song or dream in her head that she couldn't stop thinking about.

During the day, it was almost impossible to catch Gwen when she wasn't herding kids—hers and half the neighborhood's. She always had a smile. Was always dressed in practical cotton or denim. Always had time to give a neighbor a helping hand or a listening ear—including him—but he'd never seen any guy around the place except for her good-looking, cold-eyed ex.

If Spence hadn't seen her, all those moonlit nights, he would never have guessed there was more to the package than the practical single mom and commonsense neighbor. But he'd seen the sensual beauty in Gwen, the dreamer side to her... and the loneliness.

From the beginning she'd never given him more than the friendly time of day. Spence sensed she needed healing time to get over her divorce. He understood that. He had scars left over from the breakup of his marriage to May, and there was no fast recovery from certain kinds of emotional wounds.

Two years had passed, though. Two years of watching her and thinking about her and using their mutual single-parent problems to naturally create excuses to talk with her. Spence had never tried a serious move. It pushed his black humor buttons, though, that an embarrassing number of women in his business life seemed willing to chase him, given no encouragement at all, yet Gwen had never given him the first sign that she noticed he was a male human being. Maybe she didn't like brown hair and brown eyes. Maybe tall men didn't turn her on. Maybe she liked big brawny guys instead of lean. Spence had a sister who'd never treated him as sisterly as Gwen did.

She hadn't kissed him last night like a sister, though.

With his gaze still on the window view, Spence set his iced tea glass in the sink. He considered whether he was up for a knife-in-the-gut rejection. He considered how many clear no-touch signals she'd given him over the past two years. He considered that he hadn't taken a serious risk with a woman since May, and having his heart torn out had been as much fun to recover from as a bullet wound.

Spence rubbed the back of his neck, then abruptly pivoted around. He checked first on April, to make sure she was dead-to-the-world asleep, then inhaled a lungful of courage and strode determinedly for the back door.

The problem—the really nasty, unsolvable problem—was that the only way to figure out what Gwen Stanford felt—or could feel for him—was to go over there and find out.

But taking the risk sure felt like diving into the ocean with no life buoy or rescue raft in sight.

Three

"You give me fever... when you kiss me..." It was tough to belt out rock and roll when you couldn't carry a tune to save your life and had to whisper because the boys were sleeping—but brownie making wouldn't be the same without a song. Gwen cracked two eggs and plopped them in the bowl.

"I know you're gonna treat me ri-i-i-ight..." She checked the recipe for the amount of sugar. One cup. That struck her as a little stingy, so she heaped in some extra. "Louie, Louie..." Oops, she was pretty sure those were lyrics to some other oldie, but no matter. There was still a hip-swinging beat to that one, too. Only drat, she'd forgotten to preheat the oven.

Holding a wooden spoon dripping sugar and chocolate, she swiftly pivoted around... and almost had a heart attack when she saw Spence in her screen doorway. "Eek," she said weakly.

Even in the muzzy darkness beyond the screen, she could see his effort to control a smile. "Sorry, I really didn't mean to scare you. I was just about to knock— but then I decided you looked too busy for company and maybe I'd better head back home."

It took a second to gather her scattered wits... but then she grinned. "Now tell the truth. My singing just terrified you speechless, didn't it? Come in, come in. I promise I'll quit. I'll even pour you a glass of lemonade..." She glanced at her hands, spattered with chocolate and flour. "Well, maybe you'd better pour your own lemonade."

"You do look busy—"

"I am. The brownies are for Ms. Peter's class tomorrow—she's Josh's second-grade teacher, and I caught wind it was her birthday. Figured it was a good idea to start the school year by buttering her up. There's nothing more boring than making brownies by yourself, though, so I couldn't be happier to have some company. What's up? April isn't sick, is she?"

"No, she's fine, sleeping like a log." Spence stepped inside. Even in casual khakis and old sandals, he made her pulse rate accelerate to zoom speed. "She came home from school—it's only the second day, mind you—and tells me she now knows how to read. Nothing to it."

Gwen chuckled, then motioned where he could find the glasses. "There's fresh-squeezed lemonade on the first shelf in the fridge...and April's so bright, I wouldn't doubt she moved past Dick and Jane in the first fifteen minutes. What a darling she is."

"I think so, too, but actually, I heard she poured several handfuls of sand down Jacob's shirt this afternoon. I figured I'd better find out if the McKennas were in hot water at your house."

So that's why he'd stopped over? Head down, she started ladling brownie batter into the baking pan. "No problem. I found the sand when I threw Jacob in the bathtub tonight, but believe me, dirt and Jacob isn't any news to our septic system. And what's a little sand between friends? Apparently Jacob paid her the ultimate compliment by telling her she played as well as a boy. No offense meant to your gender, but I bopped him with a towel. I swear my two came out of the womb thinking sexist . . . do you want to lick the bowl?"

"Lick the bowl?"

Gwen had long suspected that the whole world treated Spence like a hotshot—because he was. She always meant to kowtow the same way and treat him like the intimidating business tycoon he was, only she'd never mastered how to do it. "Hey, it's fine with me if you're too grown-up to get your hands sticky. Personally I don't think anything beats brownie batter, but—"

"I'll take the bowl off your hands."

She chuckled. "You're gonna do me a favor, huh? But maybe this is a bad idea. You've got a white shirt on, and Mary Margaret'll skin you alive if she has to get chocolate stains out of it—"

"I'll handle Mary Margaret. I haven't had brownie batter in a dozen years."

"Well, you poor baby. . ." He hovered like a four-year-old until she had the batter poured in the pan— then promptly and greedily absconded with the bowl— and the wooden spoon. Sheesh, who'd have dreamed this would go so easily, she mused. Last night she'd been mortified at the thought of having to face him again, when obviously she only had one choice. To be herself and to act like normal.

She grabbed a soapy sponge. Something about making brownies always took out her whole kitchen. There were drips of chocolate on the pecan cupboards and a dusting of flour everywhere on the coral Formica counters. Working around Spence at the island bar, she swiped and scrubbed with the sponge. She was conscious that her feet were bare, her face as scrubbed as a kid's, and he'd probably been around women all day dressed in elegant business suits. Her oversize brown T-shirt and red shorts were ancient and looked it—but he'd seen her look worse.

Come to think of it, he'd never seen her looking anything *but* worse. At the moment she doubted he'd notice if she were wearing red satin or gold lamé. His head was buried pretty deeply in the chocolate bowl. "Good grief. Doesn't Mary Margaret ever make you brownies?"

"She bakes. We had a mystery pie last night. I didn't have the courage to ask what it was. Definitely not brownies, though. And definitely nothing like this. How's your head?"

"My head?"

"No headache? I only had one experience with dark sweet rum, way back in college, but I remembered it being pretty lethal the next morning."

She'd hoped—she'd so earnestly prayed—that he'd forgotten all about last night. "Well, I woke up this morning with a fairly good head pounder. Bad enough to convince me that if I were going to take up a vice, it'd be something besides alcohol." She added swiftly, lightly, "I can hardly remember anything that happened last night after the first sip."

"No?"

"Nope. Not a thing. I slept like the dead, though, that's for sure...." She finished her cleanup and perched on the kitchen stool next to him, still drying her hands on a watermelon-print towel. Not that she was in a hustle to change the subject, but the winning horse at the Derby couldn't have hustled any faster. "Did you have a good day? Market some good business deals?"

"Had a great day. Marketed up a storm. So...did you have any time today to shop for some Victoria's Secret underwear?"

"Beg your pardon?"

"Last night..." He frowned, as if trying to recall her exact words. For a man who'd been salivating for chocolate seconds before, suddenly he seemed to have forgotten all about the brownie bowl. "You were talking about turning over a new leaf and becoming 'reckless.' I'm pretty sure you mentioned that a shopping trip to Victoria's Secret was part of that agenda...whoops. Has Gwen disappeared on me?"

He reached over to peek under the kitchen towel she'd flopped over her head.

"Nope. She's still here," he announced gravely.

"She's hiding under the towel because she's dying of embarrassment," Gwen said dryly. "I was counting on you to be a gentleman and forget everything I said last night. I never meant any of it—"

"I thought you made all kinds of good sense."

"Good sense?" She pulled the towel off then, if only to see his face. She assumed he was pulling her leg, yet his expression—bewilderingly enough—

seemed sincere and serious. "I dipped into half my supply of cooking rum for the annual rum cakes I make around the holidays. Far as I recall, I barely swallowed the first sip before I quit making *any* sense."

"Well, I guess I came over for nothing, then, because that was exactly what I wanted to talk with you about. I thought maybe we could help each other."

"Help each other?" Gwen didn't mean to keep parroting him, but so far—beyond feeling eternally grateful that he hadn't brought up that blasted kiss— she seemed to be having a major problem following the conversation.

Spence pushed aside the bowl and lazily propped his long legs on the opposite kitchen stool. "You sounded...trapped. I understand how that feels, Gwen. My life is my daughter right now—and I don't want it any other way. But besides her and work, there doesn't seem to be any free time in a day. Single parenting is a twenty-four-hour-a-day job."

"You're not kidding," she agreed.

"But even loving it, you *can* feel trapped. At least I do, sometimes. I imagine you feel just as buried under the same mountain of single-parent responsibilities."

"I do," she agreed again, still unsure where he was leading.

"Well, I don't think it's selfish—or weird—that you feel like you need to break out sometimes. Maybe you were teasing about doing something 'reckless.' But I think it's a pretty human, healthy need to crave some time to yourself. And it occurred to me..."

"What?"

He lifted a hand in a boyish gesture. "It just occurred to me that we're both in the same boat. It's really hard for a single parent to pull off any free time—without a fellow conspirator. I'm guessing you don't hire many baby-sitters?"

"No."

He nodded. "Me, either. I've got Mary Margaret during the day for April, but I really hate leaving her with strangers in the evening just because I selfishly need some time off. I mean...I *want* to give my daughter that personal time, or at least know she's with someone who really cares about her. Strangers don't cut that mustard."

"I feel exactly the same way," Gwen said honestly. "I hate leaving the boys with baby-sitters. Even though I'm home, I'm either working—or running hard—during the day. It's not the same as real time with them, and especially because of the divorce I feel they need that time in the evenings. I just feel really selfish and guilty if I leave them."

"Yeah. I understand. But I kept thinking about how our kids play together all the time, have a good time with each other, so it's not like any of us are strangers. If we combined resources, it seems to me it could help us both. Which is to say—if you want an ally, I'm volunteering to be one."

"Well, Spence, you've got an ally right back. But I don't know exactly what you're thinking about doing...."

"I never had any set plan. I was just thinking...why don't we try something?" He shrugged his shoulders, and then as if the idea had just popped in his head, suggested, "I've got an early workday tomorrow, should be home by four. How about if you just plan to take off, do whatever you feel like doing. I'll take the kids, do dinner, keep 'em busy until bedtime.''

The thought of four hours free—actually free— danced in her head like a vision of sugarplums and gaily wrapped packages at Christmas. But a lot of years had passed since she believed in Santa. "I can't possibly ask you to do that," she informed him— and herself—firmly.

"You're not *asking* me to do anything. I'm offering. And you can offer back the same way. Hey, if it doesn't work out for the kids in a good way, we just won't do it again. But I can't see how we'll know unless we try out an experimental run, do you?"

"No," she said hesitantly.

"So we're on for tomorrow? I'll pick up your boys around four?"

"Well...okay, I guess. As far as I know, there's no reason why that timing wouldn't work out...."

She'd barely, hesitantly, agreed before Spence up and left. It was late, of course. Time for any parent of young children to be packing it in, and Spence never visited for more than a few minutes. Still, Gwen found herself at the kitchen window, hands on her hips, until he disappeared into the night's shadows.

She felt . . . odd. Her pulse was charging, her nerves kindling awareness—but that was just hormone nonsense, she suspected. Even a woman in a coma would probably notice those liquid brown eyes and that slow, wicked grin of his, and the kiss last night had naturally upped her sexual awareness quotient around Spence. No man had ever made her feel wicked before.

If she hadn't been a card-carrying Good Girl for thirty years, maybe he might have affected her less potently. But she'd liked that kiss. Liked that wicked, reckless feeling. Liked him— suddenly, personally, and way too much.

Still, her deplorable lack of control over her hormonal response to him didn't seem to completely explain the chugging, charging, uneasy beat in her pulse. Spence was turning into a serious friend. No one else, not even her sisters, understood how much or how long she'd felt trapped. Spence's perception had come as a surprise, like finding a kindred spirit, and he'd been so nonjudgmental and understanding. . . .

Abruptly the oven timer buzzed. Swiftly Gwen whisked out the brownies and set them on the rack to cool, then glanced at the clock and mentally shook her head. The boys would be raring wide awake by six-thirty. It wasn't time to think. It was time to crash. She'd be crabbier than a porcupine if she didn't catch some shut-eye.

She turned out lights, checked on her monsters, then climbed into a Miami Dolphins T-shirt and burrowed between her lemon-yellow sheets. That quickly, the whole house was dark, quiet and peaceful.

Yet she tossed. Then turned. Sleep refused to come. Those uneasy warning bells kept clanging in the back of her mind.

Spence's whole plan about helping each other sounded wonderful. She craved some free time right now. She needed the space to figure out who she was and where she was going with her life. Josh and Jacob thought Spence was "majorly cool," and likewise, she was crazy about his daughter. For fellow single parents to help each other was the best of all worlds, because they both shared the same concerns.

It was just that she felt . . . steamrollered . . . into the plan. Spence couldn't help being a dynamic, take-charge type of man. But Gwen was just coming to understand that hiding in a steamroller's shadow was exactly what she had done with Ron. It was all too easy to let a lion lead—if you were a mouse. And by making a man her whole life, she'd not only bored one husband straight into divorce court . . . she'd become boring to herself, somehow lost any concept of her own life in the process.

She needed to be careful. Infinitely careful not to fall seriously for Spence. Eventually she'd look for love again—after she mastered this independence business and learned to stand up for herself. But she already knew that she was a disastrous failure with steamrollers. Spence could never possibly work for her.

Falling for him would be her worst nightmare.

Spence decided he was going to put up his feet and read the newspaper—as soon as he quit pacing the floors. The kitchen clock read 8:20. He always had a full quota of energy, but he'd never been a nervous man. There was no earthly reason for him to be wearing a path between the kitchen, hall and living room.

The house was quiet. Dead quiet. Mary Margaret had long gone home, and all three kids had hit the sack around eight. They were already asleep. He'd checked. Josh and Jacob were camping in the spare bedroom, and April was sawing zz's on her pink pillow. The plan, in the morning, was for him to wake up the boys in time for them to flash over to their own house to get dressed for school. The boys had loved the idea of sleeping over, and that way Gwen didn't have to fret about getting home at some exact time.

She could dance until dawn if she wanted to, Spence had told her.

He'd even meant it.

Sort of.

There was no reason to expect her home, he told himself irritably. No reason to be prowling around the house when he was whipped after a long day. He could dive into the paper or a book. Pour himself a drink. Call his younger sister. Turn on his computer and work on a new advertising program that had been biting on his mind all day.

All those ideas struck him as stupendous, but he was still pacing a road between the kitchen and living room when he finally heard a sound just before nine.

She whisper-knocked on the front door and poked her head in. "Spence, are you there?" she said softly. And then she saw him in the far doorway, grinned and sprinted inside. "Were the boys good? Everything okay? How were the kids for you?"

"It went fine. They had a great time together. And you don't have to whisper—the bedrooms are in the far wing, and I looked just a couple minutes ago. All three of them are sound asleep." Once Spence got that informational chitchat out of the way, he said what was on his mind. *"Holy kamoly."*

"Uh-oh. I look weird, huh?" Gwen dropped an armful of packages in a noisy crinkle and crunch of paper, then straightened back up.

"You don't look weird."

"Too much putting on the dog? Too much makeup? Too wild...?"

The only thing "wild" Spence noticed was the wild, vulnerable uncertainty in her face. Deliberately he circled around her with narrowed eyes. As he circled, her cheeks flushed. Nervously she pulled on an earring, then the other earring...and started talking faster than he could draw breath. "I just thought it'd be fun. To have a make-over. And once I had all that new makeup on, it seemed like I might as well try a haircut and a little different hairstyle. And I haven't actually bought clothes—except for the boys—in a month of Sundays. The stores were showing a bunch of new stuff for fall...."

She finally trailed off. Spence understood he was expected to say something. And he would. As soon as he found his voice again.

He'd known she was beautiful. She just didn't have a flashy type of beauty—or any awareness of her allure. Still didn't.

But Spence did. And the changes in her tonight only put an exclamation on a declarative truth he already knew. Her hair had been short before, but now it was feathery, framing her face in soft spikes, giving her a tousled, sexy, French look. Something about her eyes looked darker, more dramatic. The new silk blouse wasn't fancy, just a blouse, but the cream color set off her golden skin and the coral cameo she had pinned at the throat. The skirt was swishy and long and cruelly hid those damn fine legs of hers, but the style was pure female. Pure *her*.

"You look stunning," he informed her seriously.

"Hardly that." But she laughed, both nervously and with a little relief in there, too. "It was kind of fun. Just...goofing off. And you'll never believe what happened."

"What?"

"These two guys whistled at me on the escalator. You know what else?"

"What?"

"Another guy tried to pick me up in the parking lot. I was just walking toward my car when he was walking toward his. When he started talking to me, I thought he was just being nice, you know, the way friendly types wander into conversations when you're stuck in lines or in elevators or wherever? But good grief, he asked me out. I almost had a heart attack."

So did Spence. "Got a taste for the reckless life, did you?"

She chuckled. "Maybe not reckless on a parachute jumper's terms, but I haven't wasted an entire afternoon since...well, since I can remember."

"Getting out was good for you."

"Yeah, it really seemed to be." She seemed surprised when he wrapped her hands around a glass of fresh-squeezed limeade. In between breakneck pacing around the house, Spence had more than enough time to make it. And since she was still hovering by the door, close to her packages, he figured she was planning on leaving lickety-split unless he did something to stall her. "I should check on the boys and go, really—"

"You're welcome to look in on the boys, but I bet it'd feel real good to kick your shoes off for a minute and relax?"

"Well..."

She was thirsty, he could see. And he didn't have to coax her that hard into crashing for a few minutes on his saddle leather couch. She even slipped off her shoes and curled her legs under her. Either the shopping or turning herself into a sexy femme fatale had clearly temporarily zapped her quota of nervous energy.

His quota of nervous energy, by contrast, had soared somewhere near the stratosphere.

He switched on the lamp behind her, creating a soft pool of cream light, and kept a steady conversation going about his activities with the kids—dinner at Ponderosa, the three-against-one soccer game in the backyard, the finger-painting marathon the monsters had put him through at the kitchen table.

He had Gwen chuckling, but he also saw her gaze absently stray around the room. She'd been in his house dozens of times, but never in the formal living room before. Both of them had always been more inclined to pop in and out of each other's kitchens for the type of casual, neighborly conversations they usually had. Now, though, she glanced around, noticing his Pakistani burgundy-and-cream rug, the Indian-carved teak coffee table, the Oriental prints on the walls and the man-size leather furniture.

Spence was pretty sure none of it went together. He bought stuff he liked—when he got around to it—but never had a clue what you were supposed to do as far as decorating. She'd know, he thought. Everything in Gwen's house was warm and comfortable and made her whole place feel like a "home." Maybe he could ask her to help him out sometime.

That seemed a good idea, but the thought wouldn't hold in his mind. Adrenaline was still pumping through his pulse at the thought of all those strange guys coming on to her. Spence couldn't have been less surprised that men noticed her...but Gwen sure as hell seemed to be.

"So...did you accept a date with that guy in the parking lot?" he asked casually.

"Are you kidding? He was a total stranger." The light trapped gold and fire in her hair when she leaned over to set down her limeade glass. She was tired, he could see from the way she cuddled back in the corner of the couch. But she was also relaxed, with a mischievous sparkle and dance in her eyes. "To tell you the truth, I was more embarrassed than anything."

"Embarrassed?"

She nodded with a wry chuckle. "Because it never occurred to me the guy was serious, I'm afraid I really bungled the conversation. I mean...I'd have just said no right away if I understood where he was going, but I didn't have a clue. I just haven't flirted in a blue moon. I'm completely out of practice. Working at home I don't meet many people, and just haven't been out much since the divorce."

"You want a coach?" he asked teasingly.

"A coach?"

Spence meant it as a joke, but when Gwen didn't immediately laugh, he hesitated. "Maybe coach is the wrong word, but...well...I do happen to know your enemy from the inside out, so to speak. It's been a lot of years since I lived in the fast lane, but I drove a lot of miles on that road. And in the business world, I'm around single predators all the time—both male and female. Dating practices are a real different ball game in the nineties."

"I'm not really thinking about dating," she assured him.

"If you're going to go around looking that beautiful, neighbor, you're going to have guys giving you a rush."

The same color whispered up her cheeks as the coral cameo at her throat. "I don't think so," she said dryly.

"I *know* so."

"Oh, God. You think I went too far with the makeup and new hairstyle and—?"

"I think you look great. I thought you looked great before. But if you're going to have some free time to get out and explore that idea about being 'reckless'—"

"Spence, I never *really* meant reckless," she said swiftly.

"Even if you only meant a *little* reckless, if this is your first time breaking out of that house since the divorce...and after being married for a number of years...you really need to be on your toes. It's a zoo out there. These days, a predator-type of man could make a pass so fast it'd make your head spin. You know what I mean?"

"Actually...no."

Spence shook his head. Sadly. "I just think you'd probably feel a lot safer if you had a little practice."

"Practice?"

Four

"**P**ractice," Spence repeated. "There are just some things you need to watch out for, Gwen. Let me give you an example." He shifted closer on the couch and lifted his hand.

"You see how innocent this looks? A guy reaches over and touches your hair. It doesn't *seem* like a pass. He just seems curious, like he's been watching the lamplight catch all that gold and shimmer in your hair, and he can't help but wonder if the texture could possibly feel as soft as it looks. It doesn't seem like anything threatening is going on here, now does it?"

"I . . ." There was a sparkle of mischievous humor in her eyes—until his fingers sieved into her hair. Spence saw her swallow, saw her eyes widen, saw her whole body become statue still.

"And then the side of his hand strays down the side of your jaw. Again, it doesn't *seem* like a pass. It just seems like this guy can't help himself from discovering how your skin feels, because it looks like cream and it's just so tempting to touch it. Still, his touch is gentle, not aggressive. Nothing to make you worry, right?''

"I..." Again, nothing emerged from her mouth but that single, lone syllable. The instant he touched her skin, her gaze riveted on his. He saw confusion in those soft brown eyes, as if she expected the humor in this "coaching lesson" to show back up any second now. But he also saw the same vulnerable shine of willingness and yearning that he'd caught in her eyes the night before.

"But you see how he's managed to maneuver close to you? When a guy is moving in on you, you can't take anything he does as innocent, Gwen. You hear me?''

"I...yes, I hear you."

"Because if he's already manipulated the situation to get this close, it's easy, real easy, for him to follow through. Like this. See?''

His lips touched down, softer than thistledown. He only intended a swift, short kiss. Guilt was harassing his conscience pretty mercilessly. Initially this "coaching" lesson had seemed easy to justify. Gwen was beyond bright, but she was also hopelessly honest by nature. Wiles and guiles were just never going to come naturally to her, and she'd really been removed from the predatory single scene for a lot of years. He didn't want her hurt. A little brotherly coaching would help her to protect herself.

His reasoning was so self-righteous and gentlemanly that damned if he knew how his conscience saw through it.

The truth was that he'd never had a single brotherly feeling for Gwen. Another nasty truth was that he'd been edgy ever since she'd mentioned that dude coming on to her in the parking lot. And another unpleasant truth was that if she wanted a taste of recklessness—right or wrong, conscience or no conscience—he didn't want any guy giving her a sample but him.

Her mouth was silken, warm. Shy warm. Tempting warm. She didn't move, didn't seem to even breathe, but her lips were vibrantly alive under his; mobile, supple. Alluring. Her eyes closed, lashes fluttering down to make satin shadows on her cheeks. Her warm skin seemed to release the perfume she was wearing, nothing musky, nothing heavy—but something innocently light and flowery like lily of the valley. It had never occurred to him before that such a vague, sweet scent could be remotely dangerous.

Now it did.

Spence was well aware that rum had likely influenced her responsiveness to him the night before. But tonight she'd had nothing but a glass of limeade. Her lips tasted of those tangy limes, of the sugar and of a spicy-sweet flavor belonging solely to her.

He never meant to deepen the kiss. And when she felt the soft, testing intrusion of his tongue, her hand shot up to stop wherever that kiss was traveling. But she didn't stop him. Her fingers landed on the cords of his neck, touched them, and then she folded a palm around his nape and pulled him closer to her.

She'd treated him like a friendly, neighborly eunuch for so long that he'd never been sure she noticed he was a man. His hand strayed to the manic pulse in her throat. Her tongue met his, slippery as a secret, matching his, matching the pressure of a kiss that had already turned dark as a storm and just as wildly tumultuous.

She noticed.

Her spine curved like a bowstring, her breasts molding to his chest. Desire bucked through him like an unruly colt. He was no stranger to desire, but physical needs and finding a woman whose response to him was honest and real and vulnerable aroused him like a devil fire. If he'd never put into words the reason he felt attracted to Gwen, it was all here. An instinct that she was special, a male gut intuition that she was totally different from any woman he knew, that she could matter like no one in his life ever had.

His palm swept down her side, skimming her ribs, sneaking over to the ripe, taut swell of one breast. He heard her breath catch. Saw her eyes shoot open, dazed and smoky.

He hadn't touched her, not really, hadn't gone near a button on her cream silk blouse, hadn't done a single forbidden thing. But it was suddenly there, that feeling of *forbidden,* of how easy it'd be to tip straight off the cliff of *reckless* and not look back. Hot, sharp desire was pumping through him like a heady drug. He loved the look in her eyes, loved touching her, could not possibly have misread the yearning, willing promise in her responsiveness to him. But she couldn't possibly know what she really felt for him this soon. And he was close, too damn close, to losing control.

He murmured, "About five minutes ago, tiger, you were supposed to bash the guy's head in."

It took a second before that registered, but he could see that some gentle, teasing humor was the right tack to take. It gave her something comfortable to handle.

"If you, um, covered that section in the coaching lesson, I missed it."

"You're kidding. Didn't I mention that part of the rules?"

"Nope."

"Well, maybe the coach needs some coaching. I could have sworn I knew this material pretty well, but to be honest, it's been a long time. And I never meant to turn into the manipulative jerk I was trying to warn you about."

"You didn't. You weren't," she said quietly, sincerely. She swallowed hard and came up with a smile. "That was quite a lesson. And you're quite a coach, McKenna. But it's definitely past time I headed home."

She flew. Flew into her shoes, flew to check on her sons, flew to scoop up her shopping packages, flew to the door. Like nothing had happened, she chattered about sending the boys home by seven-thirty in the morning, and about how it was her turn to take April next time so Spence could have his turn at having some free time. A magpie couldn't have been friendlier, but she avoided meeting his gaze directly, and she sprinted out the door as if devils were biting at her heels.

When she was gone, Spence stood in the darkness and dragged a hand through his hair.

He wasn't sure if he'd made headway... or scared her half to death.

Ditto for him. Positively he had willingly opened new doors with Gwen. But he'd tasted risk as well as promise in the possibilities. He hadn't guarded his heart all these years by mistake. Loneliness was nasty, but at least it was safe. He'd been hurt by the mistakes in love he'd made in the past.

So had she.

The risk of hurting her preyed on his mind. And Spence suddenly felt no more safe than if he were standing on a snow-topped mountain . . . in avalanche country.

Because she was expecting April anytime, Gwen had just glanced at the McKenna house when she saw their back door open. Dad and daughter both headed across the yard to her house, but April dashed ahead, her blond hair flying as she bounded across the fence. She snagged a hug from Gwen long before Spence caught up.

"Ho-boy, ho-boy. Are we gonna have fun!" April said.

"You bet we are!" Gwen released the blond moppet, who zoomed off immediately to join the other kids. At last count there were around ten—not just her two, but the regular gang from the neighborhood. Typical of a Friday after a long week of school, the devils had energy to burn. The decibel level varied from ear-piercing caterwauls to your more basic shrieks and screams.

Spence negotiated his way past the chaos and exuberant tumble of small bodies with a humorous shake of his head. "Holy kamoly. What on earth have you volunteered for?"

She chuckled. "We're going to make mango ice cream. It's a guaranteed terrible mess, but the kids really love it." Minutes before, she'd just finished finger-counting the props to make sure she had everything ready—sugar, cream of tartar, mango puree, a big lime, partially whipped heavy cream, an old-fashioned ice cream "crank" churn . . . and of

course, the garden hose. "I learned from past experience to do everything outside—not just the churn to
crank the ice cream, but spare kids' clothes and the
hose handy. My kitchen looked like the scene from a
horror movie the one time I let 'em do it in the house."

"It sounds like fun..." Spence's gaze swiveled toward her, "but also like an awful lot of work for you
to take on alone, especially with this many kids. You
sure you don't need some help?"

Gwen needed some "help" the instant he looked at
her. She was dressed appropriately for the disaster
about to happen—her oldest T-shirt and shorts, track
shoes, no makeup and a backward baseball cap to
keep her hair out of the way. She could easily compete in a fashion show for bag ladies, which Spence
could hardly miss. Yet his gaze traveled the length of
her as if a three-night-old embrace was suddenly intimately, volatilely fresh on his mind.

"No, no, I don't need any help. And I want you to
go off and have a great time—and we agreed, it's your
turn for a night off." Gwen told herself, for the zil-
lionth time, that she was imagining the way he looked
at her. Just as she would be crazy to imagine foolish
implications from a few kisses.

They'd been such good friends. Gwen didn't want
to ruin that, and she still couldn't quite understand
how, twice now, an embrace had erupted between
them out of nowhere—but she felt positive Spence
never meant anything to happen. Likely it was just
accidental. A couple of mutual moments of insanity.
She'd probably mortifyingly proved to Spence that she
did need "coaching." The difference between his sophistication and experience and her awkward bum-
bling must have been obvious to him.

There was no point being embarrassed, Gwen had decided. It had happened. If that last embrace lingered in her mind with lethal tenacity, it was because she was a goose. A goose who'd never learned to be independent enough to handle herself—which was exactly what she was trying to correct in her life right now.

"You sure ended up with a bunch of extra kids," Spence noticed.

"Yeah, I swear kids reproduce in this backyard like rabbits— I think the word spread through the grapevine about making ice cream tonight. On the other hand, it's my theory that if you're gonna ask for trouble, you might as well go for it whole hog." She added firmly, "Now don't be worried about April. I promise, she'll have a blast."

"I couldn't be less worried. She always has a great time with you."

"I'll just bring her over when she wakes up in the morning, okay? So you don't have to worry about what time you get home..." Her voice trailed off as she saw a four-year-old tumble off a swing. She started sprinting for the neighborhood tyke at the same time she heard the telephone jangle from the house.

"I'll get the phone," Spence offered.

"You don't have to—" she started to say, but Spence was already bounding through her back door. By the time she'd scooped up the tear-streaked four-year-old, he showed up back in the doorway.

Spence's hand covered the receiver. "It's your ex. You want to talk to him?"

Did a dog appreciate ticks? "Sure," she said. Still carrying the four-year-old, she took the receiver and stepped inside. Spence had to think her kitchen looked like the aftermath of a hurricane, but actually the cluttery mess was pretty well organized. It took one pan to cook and cool the sugar and tartar together, another bowl for the mango and lime mixture. Her next job was to whip the heavy cream. Once that was done, she could fold all the different ingredients together and let the kids loose with the old-fashioned churn outside.

Temporarily, though, she had no time to explain to Spence that the jungle of pots and pans and mess was necessary. Handling Gertrude—the four-year-old—and dealing with her ex on the telephone were both full-time jobs. Swiftly she washed the tears off the little one and handed her a sucker—a consolation prize for suffering a tumble—and then shooed the urchin back outside.

Making Ron disappear was never so easy. Given a choice between talking to her ex and a case of hives, Gwen would vote for the hives. Apparently the sole reason her ex called this time was to let her know that when he'd had the boys for his custody weekend, Josh had had a spot on his shirt.

"Pardon me?"

"There was a big spot under the collar, you know, of his blue shirt."

"Ron, dirt flies at Josh the instant he wakes up. He's seven years old. And you were taking them on a picnic, for heaven's sake, so what's the big deal?"

Ron sighed, heavily and deliberately. "You don't have to get all emotional. I was just trying to help you. This was a professional picnic, and I expected the kids to look nice. And if you didn't realize that shirt had a spot..."

Gwen wasn't headache prone, but when she hung up the phone, she leaned against the wall and rubbed at the sudden throbbing ache in her temples. Doctors had to be picky, she'd told herself a hundred times. It was how they were supposed to be, because even small mistakes could affect people's lives. Ron didn't *mean* to be belittling.

But like all the arguments during their marriage, they were over small nothings that somehow made Gwen feel she was to blame. Guilty. At fault. She didn't have to worry about pleasing him anymore, but conversations with him always brought back memories of her feeling like a failure, both as a wife and as a woman.

"Gwen?"

Her head whipped up to see Spence in the doorway. "I thought you'd gone—I didn't realize you were still standing there!"

"I didn't want to leave you with a yardful of trouble and a phone call to handle at the same time. Are you okay?"

She *had* been. More than okay. She'd had a great day and was full of bounce and bubbling energy over the project ahead with the children. Now she was conscious that her shoulders were sagging, and she was embarrassed that Spence had caught her rubbing her temples. "I'm afraid I don't handle my ex well," she admitted dryly. "I swear I need to take a course in assertiveness one of these days."

"You want to talk about it?"

"God, no." Swiftly she pushed off from the wall and straightened up. "Honestly, I'm fine. And I didn't mean to hold you up from wherever you were planning on going for the evening—"

He motioned to the production line of bowls and pots on her counters. "What all do you have to do to get this ice-cream thing started?"

"Actually, almost nothing. Everything's done—all I have to do is whip the cream. Won't take more than five minutes, and after that, the whole project goes outside. The kids get to do the cranking work, and I just play the decadent lady of leisure."

"Sure you do. And then a genie comes in afterward to clean up all the mess?"

"I have a couple of spare genies just for that purpose," she assured him. "Now you scoot! Go have fun!"

"Okay, okay, I'm leaving. I can tell when I'm not wanted."

Gwen chuckled at his put-on, aggrieved expression, but once he banged out the screen door, she assumed he was really gone. She promptly applied her attention to whipping the heavy cream, but paused every couple minutes to glance out the window and check on the children. Spence wasn't in sight.

After the cream was done, she folded all the other mango ingredients together in a giant bowl. The bowl was so heavy it took two hands to carry, so she used her hip to push open the screen door and cart it outside . . . and abruptly stopped dead.

Spence was still there. She'd noticed his neat, tailored shirt and dockers before, and tried not to speculate if he was dressed that way to take a woman out for a casual dinner. She specifically hadn't asked about his plans. Helping each other out didn't give her the right to pry. What he did with his free time was none of her business. And she'd had a tough enough time erasing the memory of that last embrace from her mind, without thinking about his embracing other women.

Positively, though, he was dressed too nicely to romp around with children ... and how he'd gotten roped into swinging the four-year-old Gertrude in his lap was beyond Gwen. She had to yell to be heard over the kids' symphonic din. "All right, y'all! We're ready—and everybody gets a turn at the crank, and that's a promise. But the first thing everyone has to do is wash their hands—and that means you, too, Gertrude!"

"Does that mean Mr. McKenna has to wash his hands?" Gertrude wanted to know.

"No, Mr. McKenna gets to bump this pop stand and escape this madhouse."

She met Spence's eyes, and he mouthed the words, "Thanks, and really, I'm leaving this time."

But somehow that didn't happen. For a few minutes she was just too busy to pay attention to where Spence was ... or wasn't. The stampede crashed helter-skelter into her house to wash hands in the back bathroom, then crashed helter-skelter back outside to the ice-cream churn. Gwen had set up a "draw straws" take-turn system to avoid fights, but that of course didn't work. Three bickering matches broke out before there was a prayer of exerting any order ... and then the real mess began.

Once the mixture started turning firm, the goal was to carefully remove the dasher and repack the ice cream in ice and salt to "ripen it." Only no kid in the history of ice cream making could wait for that ripening process to sample the goods. Gwen was prepared with spoons, but there was no chance of conning the monsters into using them, either. It took about an

hour and a half before the ice cream was made... and
devoured... the process being more or less simulta-
neous. Conservatively, Gwen figured that at least half
the ice cream ended up on clothes, hair and faces.

Spence was in the thick of it. Protecting him—or his
clothes—was like trying to hold back a tidal wave.
Gwen couldn't fathom why he stayed. Even less did
she expect him to have so much fun. Twice she'd
yelled over the troops' heads, "Are you *sure* you want
to be here? You're supposed to be getting time off for
yourself!"

He kept assuring her that he was leaving any minute. He just didn't do it. By the time her entire yard—
and every child in it—had a goopy, gloppy coating of
mango ice cream, Spence was holding his sides with
laughter. "Now I understand why you had the garden
hose out," he said, chuckling.

"Honestly, it's the only way. No self-respecting
parent is going to let them in a house in this shape—
and I've got dry clothes in enough kids' sizes that no
one is going to catch cold from being wet.... Josh!"

She called her oldest son over to hand him the hose.
"Josh is my quiet, responsible one—the only one I
could possibly trust with the hose," she explained to
Spence.

"Josh is quite the philosopher."

"Oh, dear," she murmured wryly.

"Yeah—those 'oh, dear' questions are his spe-
cialty, huh? The other night he hit me with Where's
God... What's *queer* mean... How come girls don't
have a penis... How do they make mirrors..."

"His questions can wear me out in fifteen minutes
flat," she said with a chuckle. "On the other hand, he

isn't half as physically rambunctious as Jacob, and I can always count on him to behave...oops."

"Perhaps not tonight," Spence said, deadpan.

Gwen galloped over to intervene before the water war escalated. Josh had turned the hose over to Jacob.... She knew from past experience that giving Jacob hose control was a disastrous mistake. Little Gertrude got splashed and started shrieking, and then the twins from down the road decided they wanted a turn at the hose "snake."

Beyond monitoring fairness and safe play, Gwen had no reason to exert any toughness. Getting wet was part of getting clean, and the monkeys were really having a blast. Once the sun dropped and the temperature turned chilly, she'd have to call it off, but as long as the evening was still warm, she was inclined to let them play...and Spence, by then, had collapsed in a far corner of the yard and was chortling with laughter at the kids' antics.

Gwen saw when April took her turn with the hose. She just never anticipated a problem. She *knew* Spence's daughter. April was a blond, blue-eyed angel, such a striking pint-size beauty that Gwen had long guessed his ex-wife must have been an incredible looker. April was a lovebug, bright and inquisitive and always sweet, a little on the shy side but easily coaxed out of her shell. Just then, though...oh, God, just then...the little sweetheart took ahold of the hose...

And aimed it full power on her dad.

Five

Her kitchen was the only cocoon of light in the house by ten o'clock. The ice-cream-making party was long over, the kids all snuggled in bed. Gwen had been weaving on her feet even thinking about tackling the daunting disaster still left in the kitchen...but then, she assumed she'd be tackling it alone.

"What the sam hill was *in* this pan?" Spence grumbled.

She peered over his shoulder. "Sugar water. Cooked—and dried on—to perfection."

"Maybe you'd have better luck with it? Nothing I'm doing seems to dent this black stuff—"

"No, no, you're doing a superb job," she assured him gravely, but she couldn't hold back an irrepressible chuckle. She often saw Spence in a business suit—she'd even seen him looking heart-stoppingly elegant in a tux. For sure he wasn't always dressed formally, but she'd never once imagined him with sleeves rolled up, hands immersed in soapy water, applying his particular brand of logical strategic analysis to the problem of scouring pans—not in her kitchen.

He turned his head. Dark eyes glowered at her. "Are you laughing at me?"

"Not laughing. Charmed. Back when, it used to be a hero's job to rescue the princess from the dragon...but even when I was a kid, I thought it took a *real* hero to volunteer for KP duty."

"Now there's a compliment designed to swell a man's head...assuming he was so dumb he couldn't recognize the con job. You *really* don't want to get stuck with this pan, do you?"

"God, no." Yet another chortle escaped her. Maybe tiredness was making her slaphappy, but Gwen couldn't help but notice this was how it'd been with Spence before—easy, companionable, natural. Until that stupid chemistry had reared its ugly head.

Her sudden gamboling pulse seemed to think she'd love another sample of those reckless kisses from Spence. She grabbed a broom, thinking that she'd better sweep that pang of longing into a mental dustpan. She started sweeping up a storm. She'd never believed he felt anything for her but friendship—and being able to laugh with him again felt wonderful.

"*What* are you giggling about *now?*" Spence did an actor's job of sounding aggrieved.

"I can't help it. I started to think about the shocked look on your face when April turned the hose on you... I'd have given gold to have had a camera. You were *so* drenched, so fast, and your daughter was laughing *so* hard she was rolling on the ground. And how many times did you tell me you were *leaving?*"

"Well, I kept meaning to leave." He held out a soapy hand and waggled his fingers. Gwen interpreted that to mean he wanted another weapon for the pan, so she handed him a can of scouring powder. "I had big plans for my free evening. *Big* plans. I had this superb idea of claiming a couple quiet hours to just read, put my feet up, no interruptions, no noise. But I dunno. Mango ice cream—and a soaking—proved to be definitely a more memorable experience."

Gwen's eyebrows shot up. "You were going to read? On your free, wild, can-do-anything-you-want evening off?"

"What can I say. Books are my secret vice, and I don't get to indulge too often. A lot of evenings I'm stuck bringing work home." He glanced at her. "You're surprised I like to read?"

"No, no...it's just I thought you might have planned something different for the evening." Like a sultry brunette. Or a sophisticated blonde. Not that Gwen would have voiced those thoughts aloud. "Mostly, I guess I was just surprised that you'd think an evening with the kids and the mess and the chaos would be, well...fun."

Spence lifted the blackened pan to the light, sighed and dunked it back in the water. For a minute he scrubbed in silence, as if nothing had ever devoured his attention more than that pan. But then slowly, deliberately, he started talking.

"My idea of what's 'fun' has changed a lot over the years. I used to drink hard and play hard. In fact, I met May—my ex-wife—when I was twenty-two. In a bar."

Gwen had corralled a minimountain of debris for the dustpan, but now she whisked a peek at his face.

He'd never volunteered much information about his ex-wife before.

"I didn't own any marketing business then, barely owned the clothes on my back. I had a fresh college degree and was just getting my feet wet in life—and work. There was a neighborhood bar where hotshot yuppies hung out after the workday. If you look at April, you can pretty well guess what May looked like. Blond, blue-eyed—"

"Beautiful," Gwen supplied.

"Beautiful enough to have me bug-eyed," Spence said dryly. "It was a singles hunt-and-chase bar, everyone in there young, living fast, in a big hustle. I'm not sure who picked who up. May would flirt with anyone in pants...she was a sharp dresser, a sharp looker, as aggressive and ambitious as any of the guys, full of hell. She was exactly the kind of woman I was always attracted to, the kind I always thought I'd end up being married to."

"And you did marry her." Gwen swept a broomful into the dustpan, then vaguely realized she'd swept up nothing but air. The little mountain of dust was three inches away. She wasn't paying any attention.

"Yeah, we got married. And we lived the same way married that we did single. Climbing the corporate ladder during the day, hitting the bars after work, partying hard on the weekends, keeping up with a real fast crowd. Until we, um, goofed...and she ended up pregnant."

Gwen gave up sweeping. She just couldn't seem to give a damn about the dust pile on the floor. "She didn't want the baby? Or you didn't?"

Spence studied the enemy pan again, then coated the sucker with a fresh layer of scouring powder. "I hadn't been off the high-speed roller coaster long enough to really think about what I wanted long-term. But May—she said she was 'okay' with it, but every day into the pregnancy, things got worse. She liked that fast lane. She liked to flirt. She liked to hustle. April was two months old when she packed a bag in the middle of the night and left."

"She literally left you and the baby? Just like that?" Gwen asked softly.

"Yup. Never contested the divorce or my right to full custody. She wrote twice. Both times she sent a solid chunk of money for April's future—I've got money now, but I was struggling financially back then. Anyway, I really don't have any idea where she is anymore. As far as I know, she's still flirting with guys in bars." He added swiftly, "Just in the last year, April started asking some questions. Beats me how I'm supposed to handle this. So far, I said that her mom and I were divorced, that I loved her so much I wanted her with me, and that her mother worked really far away—too far away to visit."

"That's a tough problem to handle," Gwen said.

Spence nodded. "At first I thought maybe it'd be easier—and better—if she thought her mom had died. I guess that sounds terrible. But I just hated the idea of April finding out that her mother walked out, rejected her. I'm not much on lies, though. Too many can come back to haunt you...and I really don't know if May will ever show up in her life again."

"I think you handled it right," Gwen said honestly.

"Thanks. And I really mean thanks. I'd been meaning to ask your single-mom advice on that. It had really been bothering me..." He turned around to face her. "Anyway, we started this conversation talking about 'fun.' That used to be my definition of fun—running with a fast crowd, hanging out in bars. And I guess you could say I got exactly what I was asking for. May was bright and beautiful, but shallow. And so was I, in those years. About as shallow and self-centered as you could get."

"I think you're being awfully hard on yourself."

"There was a time I needed to be hard on myself. I needed to change. I just wish I'd learned a whole lot younger that *real* fun was making mango ice cream."

His eyes seemed like lasers on hers when he said *real* fun, as if to be sure she was paying attention. Gwen was listening. Her mind was just spinning, trying to imagine the kind of woman who could walk out on a baby, what that desertion must have done to Spence's life—and his heart—and how few people she knew who readily owned up to the mistakes they'd made.

And then her mind stopped spinning. In the breadth of a second, she noticed the sudden silence in the yellow-lit kitchen. She noticed the hank of hair on his brow, how the muscles in his shoulders suddenly seemed stretched taut, how the smile on his mouth was fading. His eyes held hers. She wasn't sure the Jaws of Life could have broken that hold. His eyes were deep and dark, compelling, arresting, intent on her face like a hot, hot light on a cold, cold night. He took a step closer.

"Gwen?"

He *couldn't* have wanted to kiss her again. Gwen knew she was being crazy to even think such foolishness. Maybe his May had been a turkey, but there were plenty of mover-and-shaker women out there with some real character. Den moms and homemakers couldn't possibly seriously attract him. And that was a good thing, because Gwen had bored one husband into divorce court with her homebody ways. She simply couldn't—wouldn't—fall for an overpowering, overwhelming kind of man again. Ever again.

Spence took another step closer. And his eyes dropped to her mouth. And suddenly she couldn't breath for gold. "Gwen?" he repeated.

"Hmm?"

"Your pan's clean." He reached out—but only to hand her the pan.

Long after he'd left and crossed the yard to his own house, Gwen was scowling hard, rubbing her cold arms, trying to make a whit of sense out of that sudden, slow, devil's smile of his.

The morning had started out a gorilla, then gone downhill. Nothing was going well—especially not her work. Gwen figured if she got any further behind, she'd be chasing her tail into yesterday. Fretfully her fingers flew across the keyboard. Columns of figures flashed on her computer screen.

The figures belonged to Dr. Swisher. Most of her accounting clients were docs. She'd started the business when Ron was in medical school—one of them had to bring in peanut butter money—and she discovered a made-to-order clientele. All Ron's friends had been medical people, all high academic achievers, brilliant, skilled and dedicated. Six-syllable words rolled off their tongues, always making her feel inadequate and uneducated and stupid by comparison. But most of them couldn't wipe their financial noses without help. She did their payroll, their taxes, paid their bills if they wanted. It was a living.

Gwen punched in another row of numbers. Her mood was about as cheerful as a cyclone's. Dr. Swisher couldn't seem to get it through his brilliant head that it wasn't wise to spend $30,000 a month when you were only taking in $25,000. She would handle it with him. All it took was a bunch of stupid kowtowing and tact.

Undoubtedly all jobs required a certain amount of kowtowing and tact. It just depressed Gwen that she was so good at it. She'd never have started this blithering career if she hadn't been catering to Ron's needs. She'd never have built up a clientele if she hadn't been great at soothing and smoothing maestro male egos.

Taking care of other people seemed to be the only thing she'd ever done. Maybe being a caretaker wasn't the worst personality characteristic on earth, but Gwen had a bad feeling she could have been reincarnated as a rug or a doormat and nobody would ever notice the difference. Including her.

When the telephone jangled, she grabbed it impatiently with one hand, the other still tapping out numbers on the keyboard. Her older sister was on the line. "I love you, Abby, but I can't talk now. I've got work backed up to Atlanta and back."

"Gotcha. Just wanted to know if you wore the dress I gave you for your birthday yet?"

"Not yet, but that doesn't mean I'm not crazy about it—it's the most beautiful dress I've ever owned." She closed her eyes for a second, mentally picturing Abby. She'd never understood either of her sisters—and never had to, to fiercely love them. Abby, though, couldn't be more her opposite. Strikingly beautiful, poised and confident, she'd practically come out of the womb a budding business tycoon, with an exuberant, natural abundance of ambition and drive. "How's life going for you, sweets?"

"Fine, fine, five hundred irons in the fire, nothing new . . . except for a promotion coming up on the table. It's a big one."

"Are you worried about it?" Gwen asked quickly.

"Well, it's turned into a longer and bigger battle than I thought . . . but you know me, battles are my bread and butter. It wouldn't be any fun if I didn't have to fight for it."

"I can hear the excitement in your voice." But Gwen frowned. Her sister had always thrilled and thrived on challenges, but in the past few months, Abby had increasingly sounded . . . pressured. Frantic and exhausted, no matter how happy she claimed to be with her high-powered job. "Are you taking care of yourself? Eating right? Getting enough sleep?"

"Yeah, Mama Gwen," Abby teased. "Listen, you—I'll let you go if you're busy, but I want you to wear that dress, you hear me? I want you to get out of that house and spring loose from my favorite nephews and go have *fun*."

"Yes, ma'am." Gwen kept punching numbers. She'd heard parts of this lecture before. From both sisters. Incessantly.

"It's time you put that son of a rat behind you. There are a thousand men out there who'd appreciate you, but you're not gonna find any of them in that damned house."

For one brief millisecond, Gwen was tempted to mention Spence. If anyone could give her advice on a dynamite of energy like Spence, it had to be Abby. But Gwen swiftly changed her mind. Abby might have years of experience with dynamite men, but bringing up any man, in any context, would undoubtedly arouse six miles of questions that Gwen wasn't ready to answer.

"Hey, are you still there?" Abby asked.

"I'm still here. I was just thinking—what on earth would I do with a thousand men?" she asked wryly.

"Have an unbeatable amount of fun."

Abby's ready answer made Gwen chuckle, but as she hung up, she was mentally shaking her head. Her sister's response to any problem was to leap into action. Given any excuse to take charge, Abby would undoubtedly efficiently reform her clothes, her house, her attitude and anything else.

Gwen remembered how easy it had been growing up to follow Abby's forceful lead. It had always been even easier to get sucked into Ron's shadow, who was even more of a steamroller. But her real problem, Gwen recognized honestly, was not the steamrollers in life—many of whom she deeply loved. It was her. Nobody *made* her lose Gwen. Nobody made her be the steamrollee.

If she'd turned into a gutless, dependent mouse, she had only herself to blame.

The telephone rang again... and, totally exasperated now, she yanked at the receiver. A telemarketer wanted to give her a free estimate on new windows. She got rid of him.

The next call was from an insurance salesman. She got rid of him. The next call was from the cops, wanting her to contribute to their annual fund drive. Then the neighbor across the street wanted her recipe for garbanzo soup.

She *had* an answering machine. She just never used it when the children were in school, because she was always afraid the boys might need her. When the phone rang yet again, though, she was buckets more behind and feeling more frazzled than a wet cat.

"Gwen?"

"Yeah, this is Gwen." She knew her voice sounded like a loaded pistol of impatience. She couldn't help it.

"I didn't recognize you for a second, dear. This is Mary Margaret. Listen, I'm sorry to trouble you—"

"That's okay, that's okay. What's wrong?" Gwen buried her frustration. She knew Spence's grandmotherly Spanish housekeeper well enough to know the quaver in the older woman's voice was in no way typical.

"Well, the thing is that Mr. McKenna is working out of town today. He's at some construction site for a new building, something he's planning some advertising project for...and I have his car phone number, but he's not answering, and I don't believe there's any chance of his being home before five—"

Gwen kept hearing the quaver in the older woman's voice and cut to the chase. "Just tell me what's wrong, okay?"

"The school called. April fell on the playground and hit her head. She's supposed to be okay, but I don't know, and I can't reach Mr. McKenna, and my son drove me today because my car's in the shop, so this is one of the few days I just have no way to pick her up—"

"Hey, hey, calm down, it's okay. I'll go get her right now."

"Gwen, I don't know if she needs a doctor, but I could hear her crying in the school office—"

"What I'm hearing is how upset you are. Just take it easy. We'll do whatever we have to do. I'm on my way—I'm going to pick up the name of Spence's pediatrician from you first, also see if you can find his health insurance stuff just in case, all right?''

It took her two seconds to shut off the computer and find shoes, a good five minutes to stop at Spence's house and reassure Mary Margaret again, and then there was just the pedal-to-the-metal drive to the school.

April was in the school office. Her pink jeans had grass stains; her face had tear tracks; and the lump on her scalp was half the size of a golf ball. She curled up in Gwen's arms like a nesting bird, hardly taking a breath before dramatically recounting the whole accident...the kids had been playing King of the Mountain on the monkey bars during recess, and then that stupid Jimmy Greenfinch said she was too sissy to walk across the bars with her hands behind her back, so she'd showed him. And then somebody yelled and the sound scared her. And then she fell. And then she was knocked out, just like on TV. And then she woke up, and her head hurt *real* bad, so bad that when she'd got up to punch Jimmy Greenfinch she'd fallen down again.

April told most of the pitiful tale from the snuggling depths of Gwen's lap. The child was clinging tighter than a monkey as Gwen exchanged glances with both the school nurse and the principal and then grabbed for the office telephone. She tried Spence's car phone number, but there was still no answer. Damned if she knew what Spence wanted done in such a situation, but Gwen saw no choice but to do what she'd do for her own kids.

She called April's pediatrician, relayed the accident and then told the school principal she was taking the little one to the ER for an X ray. Because they lived so close, she and Spence had already listed each other as emergency numbers for the school, so she already had technical permission to take April. The principal, Mr. Bartholomew, not only agreed but expressed concern about the school's liability; he just wouldn't feel right until the child had seen a doctor. Even the school secretary put in a positive vote. Everyone thought the plan was hunky-dory... except for the angel with the big blue eyes and her daddy's pugnacious chin.

"Forget it. I'm not goin' to any doctor. I don't want any shots."

"An X ray isn't a shot, sweetheart. It doesn't hurt at all," Gwen started to explain.

"I don't want to see any doctor! I want my daddy. And I want him *now*."

So did Gwen. *Want* was a word she was trying to obliterate from any context with Spence, but sheesh, this was different.

"You can't make me go to any doctor! Or I'll hate you and never love you again as long as I live! I'm not goin' anywhere without my daddy!"

Not that Gwen's two sons weren't the best children on earth, but as it happened, she'd witnessed a few full-blown temper tantrums before. Girls, she discovered, were better at it. April had a gift for drama, for volume, for rip-your-heart-out tears, for begging, for making you feel dirt mean for doing what you had to do.

A sing-along piggyback ride got the child as far as the car. After that, Gwen moved straight to bribes— promises of suckers and of marshmallow sundaes with chocolate ice cream and of two Chutes and Ladders games as soon as they got home. Ah, hell, Gwen would have promised her the moon and sun both by the time they were halfway through the emergency room visit.

Playing straight to April's worst fear, a finger stab for blood was ordered. Gwen conned the hematologist into stabbing *her* finger first, which April thought was wonderful—until it was her turn. Then they had to wait. Forever. Then the X-ray technician was a patronizing type who thought it was stupid when Gwen insisted on initially lying on the table with April so she could explain to the child what was going to happen. After that, Gwen exhausted her entire repertoire of knock-knock jokes on the forever wait to see the doctor. The finale, more than two hours later, was handling the school insurance information and Spence's insurance information and the billing, while she was trying to juggle a purse and fifty-some pounds of a squirming, fractious April.

By then a solid knot of anxiety had taken root in her stomach. The medical report couldn't have been better. No concussion. No skull fracture. Just a plain old bump. But April sure wasn't happy with her, and Gwen wasn't sure what Spence was going to think—or say—about putting his daughter through a monstrously awful ordeal for what amounted to absolutely nothing.

Spence knocked on her screened back door. When he heard no answer, he poked his head in. The sink light glowed on the coral Formica counters, but otherwise there was no sign of life in the kitchen.

"Gwen?" He kept his voice down because it was past nine-thirty, and her sons had to be sleeping by now. For the same reason, though, he knew she had to be home.

He pushed off his shoes and padded barefoot as far as the doorway. Off to the left was her long, narrow Florida room, decorated in greens and whites and toys. The toys were winning. Even in the shadows, he could see that games and books reproduced as fast in her house as his.

"Gwen?" He wouldn't have gone farther if he hadn't spotted her. But she was there, in the far corner of the room that she'd converted into a U-shaped office. Her computer screen was on, and she was concentrating so hard that she apparently didn't hear him.

A single lamp illuminated the back of her head. Her hair looked like a tea gold halo in that soft light, and her slim shoulders were tense, encased in an oversize sweatshirt that drooped like a sigh at her nape. She was sitting on one leg. Bare toes peeked out under her fanny. Spence had no idea if she had to burn the midnight oil this late often, but the look of her cuddled up in that chair aroused something he hadn't felt in a long time.

Protectiveness, he told himself. But he knew better. The urge to sweep her out of that chair had nothing to do with protectiveness.

Again he said, "Gwen," gently, not wanting to scare her. When she still didn't answer, he came up behind her and set a bottle of Madeira on her desk.

Her eyes shot up then. Her face was silvered in the monitor light, scrubbed clean of makeup, and her eyes had the softness of melted chocolate but looked dead tired. Spence had a sudden terrifying measure of how fast he was falling. She really wasn't looking her best, yet at some point her face had become his standard of beauty, because beauty seemed to be the only damned thing he saw. "I owe you more than a bottle of Madeira for taking on April today."

"I was hoping you'd catch a minute to call or pop over to let me know how she was doing," Gwen admitted.

"She's fine. More than fine. Exhausted me and Mary Margaret both before bedtime, playing us up for sympathy, and I already know what you went through. I've taken my angel to the doc's before. She's as much fun to handle as a python."

Gwen's chuckle was low and throaty. "I admit she gave me a little hell. On the other hand, I'd love to be six years old again and have the right to pitch a tantrum at the doc's. I'm sorry I put her through it, though, Spence. As it turned out, the whole trip to the emergency room was unnecessary. But I just get really nervous around head injuries—"

"So do I. And I'd have done exactly the same thing. I'm just sorry you were stuck in the hot seat. Hell. I'm not always in the office, but there can't be two days in a year when I'm not reachable by phone. And Mary Margaret always has a car, just bad luck hers was in a mechanic's hands today. I know we put each other down as emergency numbers for the school, but I think we were both anticipating problems like rides and rain days or just some schedule change. I never expected you'd be stuck with something like this, but I have to say, I'm really glad you were there for her."

"Hey, there's no way single working parents don't get in a bind sometimes. I know you'd have done the same for me, and I...um...what are you doing?"

Spence thought it was pretty obvious what he was doing. He'd stepped behind her and was slowly initiating a serious back and neck rub. "This is part of the thank-you. Don't give me any grief. I'm feeling bad enough—pretty obvious you're working late because of April taking so much of your time today."

"You don't have to do that—"

"Are you ever tense. You've got some muscles knotted tighter than a coiled-up Slinky back here. Put your head down."

"No, really, I—"

She said no—but her head flopped forward like a rag doll's. His fingertips attacked the muscles in her neck, then knuckled and kneaded his way to her shoulders. Her skin was warm under his hands. Supple. But she sure wasn't giving up those knots very easily. "How the hell long have you been working on that computer?"

"Ten years too long," she murmured.

He'd expected more of a sane answer—something in hours, not years. But then, like a little mental light bulb flash, he realized she was telling him how long she'd been doing this kind of work...and how she felt about her job. "Well, that's what this feels like—ten years of backed up knots. This may take a while. Put your head back."

"No."

Her no's, he noticed, were getting weaker. "You're kidding me. You're turning down a scalp rub? I've never met a human being alive with the strength of character to turn down a scalp rub. I'm in awe."

"You won't be in awe if your neighbor melts down into a pile of gelatin right in front of your eyes."

He grinned. "I can live with this threat. Close your eyes, tiger. You played Super Mom all day—partly because of my kid—so it'd be pretty mean not to let me pay you back. Listen to Dr. McKenna. It's time for you to relax.''

"Uh, Spence? I don't play doctor with grown-ups."

"Well, damn. Why not? I always thought the game was wasted on kids. It's a lot more fun when you're over twenty-one."

She chuckled, but there was a catch of uneasiness in her chuckle. Uneasiness...and excitement. His fingers sieved into her hair, rubbing, stroking into her scalp, her silky hair folding around his hands. He leaned her head back against his abdomen so he could rub her forehead, her temples.

From nowhere she suddenly shivered. It wasn't cool in the Florida room. If anything, it was hot under the glare of lamplight. The charge between his fingers and her skin seemed to be gaining warmth, sensuality, electric awareness. She was both loosening up and tensing at the same time.

So was he. Considering he hadn't touched a single intimate part on her body, Spence wasn't sure how he'd gotten aroused so hard, so fast. The problem seemed directly related to the mystifying scents of baby powder and strawberry shampoo—or the way his mind instinctively connected those scents with her. His hands drifted down to her jaw, still stroking, still gently rubbing. With her head tilted back, he had a rogue's view of the soft swell of her breasts, ripe, full, rising and falling with each breath. If his hands traveled just a few more inches downward, his fingers could deliver a full body rub where it mattered.

He wanted to.

He wanted to know what her breasts would feel like, cupped in his palms, wanted to know precisely what it took to turn her oven button to Broil and please her.

From there, it was an easy leap to wondering what she'd feel like stretched next to him between cool, soft sheets, naked, those taut, full breasts free for him to claim, her body his to tease and torment... and pleasure.

"Hmm," she said helplessly.

Spence swallowed. That was precisely the sound that he would love to hear from her—in a slightly different setting and context. His mind scrambled for control. He remembered finding an abandoned kitten when he was a kid... he'd brought the kitten a saucer of milk but the creature was too wild and scared of him to come closer... he'd gotten impatient and tried to grab her, thinking he was helping, but the kitten had run like wind then. Because he'd scared her, he'd lost her.

Spence sensed Gwen was wild and wary the same way, her ability to trust battered by the overbearing jerk she'd been married to. If he moved too fast, he risked her running. Still, his blood was rushing, his heartbeat tuned only to her channel, and every temptation in that heartbeat was thrumming, heady and heavy. If she said "Hmm" one more time, he just couldn't guarantee being responsible....

"Hmm," she said helplessly.

Six

"*Work,*" Spence snapped.

"Work?" Gwen's voice was vague. Her eyelashes fluttered up as if she were sleepily waking from a dream.

"Yeah. Work. Your work." He heard himself stuttering around like a teenage boy. His gaze pounced on the figures on the computer monitor as if they were life buoys and he was drowning. He pried his fingers off her body one by one and jammed those misbehaving hands safely in his pockets. "A few minutes ago you said something about being stuck on the computer ten years too long. That's how long you'd been doing this kind of bookkeeping work? You don't like it?"

Spence wasn't sure how they ended up still talking at two in the morning. At some point they'd meandered into the kitchen. At some point she'd put a plate of cookies on the table, then some peanuts; then she'd opened the Madeira. Neither of them had more than a glass, but they were both punch-drunk from exhaustion. Because Mary Margaret had stayed overnight, he didn't have to worry about April being alone, but Gwen was as sleepy and beat as he was.

Still, maybe it was tiredness that softened her defenses. She'd never opened up with him this easily before, and no matter how late the hour, he didn't want to shut down the conversation.

"So what *are* you doing in a field you hate so much?"

"It's not that easy to explain, Spence. I got into it because it worked. It paid good money, and at the time, Ron was in medical school and I pretty much needed to support us. Also the kids were babies then, and I really wanted work I could do at home. It seemed like a perfect job—"

"Not if you hate numbers, it isn't."

Gwen pulled up her knees and snuggled her arms around them. "That's part of what's killing me. That this is all I've done, the only job I really know, and I've wasted all this time doing something I really hate. I haven't done anything with my life. I haven't even tried to explore anything else. God, Spence, I'm such a mouse."

"You're not a mouse, you doofus. Quit calling yourself that."

"But I'm trying to be honest with myself. I don't want to be a dependent type of person anymore. I made Ron my whole life. That wasn't his fault, it was mine. But I don't want to repeat the same kind of mistakes again. I want to stand up on my own. I want to be ... tough."

Tough. This, from the lady with the silky hair and the butter-soft eyes who poured love into everyone around her. "Okay. So you want to be tough. Give me an example. Let's get specific here."

"Well—" she thought for a few seconds "—Ron tends to be on the manipulative side. I have no reason to talk with him except about the kids, but I'm still watching myself get sucked in."

"Sounds like we'd better get a serious down-and-dirty list going here." Spence grabbed a scratch pad and a ballpoint pen, making her roll her eyes and chuckle—but he was taking her seriously, and even if she was a little embarrassed, she seemed to know it. "Okay. You want some assertiveness techniques on how to handle your ex...."

"Yeah. For starters. And I'd like to at least get out there and see if there are some other possible careers that I could try."

"Okay. You need some freedom and spare time to look into that. Take some managing to pull it off, but definitely in the 'can do' column."

She sighed dryly. "Then I need the guts to go for it. Rashly assuming I find a different job, of course."

"Okay. You need some guts." He gravely scribbled that one in block letters. "Maybe we can find some guts on sale at the local convenience store? Now what else?" He lifted his head. "Are we still looking for, um, some 'reckless' opportunities?"

She smiled, but her jaw had a definite upward tilt. No question it was a stubborn smile. "Yeah. I know it sounds stupid and maybe even irresponsible—"

"No, it doesn't."

"It's just that...I don't even know what freedom tastes like. I've had this scary feeling for months now, like I'm lost, like I don't even know who Gwen Stanford is. I've been a wife and a mom and a daughter and a friend. It's not like I didn't *want* to be those things, but they were always roles defined by other people. You probably can't understand what I'm talking about—"

"Hey, tiger, I don't have to understand a damn thing. This is *your* list."

"Well, I think one reason my marriage failed and I'm feeling so dissatisfied with my life is at least partly because I left 'me' out of the equation. Out of the decision-making process, out of the action. I'm sick, sick, sick of being a so-called good girl, Spence."

"No more Ms. Nice Girl," Spence wrote down.

"I'm bored with me."

"Just going on record—no one else is," he mentioned, but she was already moving on.

"My best life skill seems to be kowtowing. How disgusting is that?"

Spence clicked on his ballpoint pen again. "Learn to kick butt. Develop antiterrorist manual to cope with bullies. No more kowtowing."

Finally a full-fledged peal of a giggle from her. For a delicious long moment, her eyes rested on his, warmer than sunlight. "I don't know why you're not laughing at me. This all has to sound silly to you. I think you'd like especially my one sister, Abby. She's got the same kind of go-getter energy that you do, just a natural abundance of ambition and drive. I don't think you could even remotely imagine being a mouse."

"Well, I don't happen to see you as a mouse. On the other hand, you want some lessons in assertiveness, some coaching about kicking butt...you're talking up my alley there." It really was late—beyond late. But he carefully pocketed that secret list of hers before standing up and then saying quietly, "When May left me, my self-esteem was lower than the bottom of a well. You think I can't understand what you're going through?"

"Can you?"

"It was like being in a room where I couldn't escape the mirrors. I knew where the fault was mine. But knowing that and fixing me were two different things."

Her eyes widened in surprise. "Yes. Exactly."

"I was afraid to even consider another relationship. Before doing that, I wanted proof in blood first that I'd changed enough to not make the same mistakes. I had to feel . . . pride again. Pride in myself."

"Oh, God, Spence. You *do* know."

Yeah, he knew. A few minutes later, as he walked home across the yard, his shoulders were hunched in thought. The grass was spiky and wet, sweet scents drifted from her lush flower beds, but thick clouds scuttled across the moon, making it difficult to see for the shadows.

He really did know about the kind of shadows that troubled Gwen. He knew precisely how a failed marriage could cripple your pride and self-respect. He understood how she'd been cornered by so many responsibilities that she felt trapped.

But she was singing an awfully clear song about needing freedom. And walking in that rough velvet darkness, Spence was painfully reminded that he'd lost his heart before to a woman who wanted freedom more than him.

It wasn't the same, he told himself. He swore he'd never get involved with another woman who didn't value commitment, but his ex-wife was nothing like Gwen. Gwen had been badly burned. With the right love, both partners felt more free—not less. They made things possible for each other. They didn't put a noose around each other's necks.

And those were things he could show Gwen...he even had the means to do that. As Spence reached the back door, he patted the the crinkle of paper in his shirt pocket. Gwen had laughed when he was making that list—and he'd been trying to make her laugh—but everything on that list was damned serious, concrete ways he could help her.

Helping her break out and fly free, though, had a giant ironic risk attached. He was ransoming his heart on the hope she'd see him as the kind of lover who would never cage her...but she could just as well choose to fly straight for freedom and away from the noose of any man. There was no way to know where her heart stood—except by risking his own.

On her new career search, Gwen considered plumbing. Master plumbers hauled it in pretty good. She was already an ace-pro at leaky faucets, once conquered a disaster with frozen pipes, knew her way around washers and Allen wrenches. But then there was the unpleasant side of plumbing.

With her jaw clamped in concentration, she put shoulder power into working the plunger again. Suck, pull. Suck, pull. Heaven knew what the boys put down the john this time, but she'd bet the bank it was something different than what was supposed to be flushed. Thankfully—this time—there was no "you know what" to clean up, but the water spilling and splashing all over her bathroom was still a royal mess.

On the millionth try, the plunger coaxed loose a gruesome neon orange plastic spider—definitely Jacob's. Since that needed to be sanitized in bleach, Gwen figured she might as well give the boys' bathroom a bleach overhaul, too.

Her hands were dryer than wrinkled prunes and she was just carrying the bucket to the laundry room when she heard a strange sound outside. An engine sound. And naturally car engines vroomed occasionally through the neighborhood all day, but this was sort of a revved-up, spicy, vroom sound, almost like a motorcyle. And it sounded so close. Almost in her driveway.

Just from curiousity she glanced out the window— and almost dropped the bleach bucket.

There *was* a cycle in her driveway. A monster black-and-chrome Harley-Davidson, gleaming like sin in the midday sun.

A thundering knock on her door followed. Thoroughly bewildered, she grabbed a towel to dry her hands and hustled for the door. Spence stood there, wearing a gray pin-striped suit, business shoes and a blue-and-gray-striped tie. He looked very much the business tycoon at his most lethal...except for the two motorcycle helmets under his arms.

"Have you had lunch?"

"Lunch?" The word might as well be in a foreign language. She peered over his side again at the Harley. "Have you lost your mind, or am I hallucinating?" she asked delicately.

"I had a feeling you'd like that set of wheels," Spence said with satisfaction. "And not to worry.

Mary Margaret's on alert if any of our urchins call from school. All you need is shoes."

"Lunch? Shoes?" She didn't mean to play parrot, but the last she'd noticed, her jeans were damp at the knees, her feet were bare, her hair hadn't seen a brush in hours, and she had to smell like bleach. Any sane man would be ashamed to be seen in public with her— hells bells, *she'd* be ashamed to be seen with her. Spence took a dawdling head-to-toe round-trip and met her eyes with a rogue's twinkle. "You're ill," she said with concern.

"Never felt better," he said, correcting her.

"No flu? No fever or chills? No—"

"Ms. Stanford," Spence said formally, "I do believe you're the lady who confessed to a teensy pining for recklessness. Now, you're being kidnapped for lunch and that's that. No matter how much work you've got—or I've got—we both have to eat. The sun's hot, the wind's wild, lunch is already packed on the back of the cycle and I won't take no for an answer."

She looked straight into his dark, sexy eyes—but nobody sane seemed to be home, and it was extremely hard to argue logic with the demented. He gave her two minutes—clocked—to change clothes.

The next thing she knew, she was straddling the cycle, her arms wrapped around Spence, laughing from the sheer joy and exhilaration of the fast ride...and of being with him. Impulse seemed to build like a tumbleweed. She didn't forget her life or her kids— there was never a moment she forgot her sons. But spontaneity had been so badly missing from her life, and being with Spence somehow made her feel reckless, wild, more exciting than she really was. It was like dipping into a fantasy that she didn't have to worry was too real.

Spence parked the cycle in the sheltered lee of a dune off the St. Augustine beach. In the middle of a workday, the only bodies around were a few tourists, dawdling down the beach as they collected shells. Gulls called and cried. White-gold sands sifted colors in the glazing bright sun. Frothy, bubbly waves glistened like aquamarines. Spence unruffled a blanket for their table and laid out a feast. All St. Augustine historical specialties, he told her—orange wine, shrimp with a lemon caper sauce, oyster devils, key lime pie.

Gwen had no idea what put the nonsense in his mood today, but his brand of madness was hopelessly infectious. He was having such a dramatic good time serving his goodies that she couldn't help but laugh. "Although I don't know about the oysters, Spence. I've never tried those."

"Hey, have I fed you any poison yet?" Both of them had pushed off shoes and were sitting cross-legged on the blanket. She could have looked at Spence all day, his formal white shirt and tie so incongruous with his bare feet, his hair ruffling in the tangy breeze ... but she wasn't sure about the little thing on the fork he was aiming for her mouth.

"No, but oysters are ... well ... oysters."

"Close your eyes, Ms. Stanford. Try it like the reckless woman you are." He slipped the delicacy between her parted lips, then waited. She tasted, then chewed, then swallowed.

"Heavens," she murmured. "If this isn't a measure of how having no guts can goof up your life. I can't believe I never tried these before. As of right now, they just showed up on my must-indulge list—"

"Uh-oh. Maybe I'd better mention a small problem with oysters." Spence faked a sober expression... as he served her another one. "Remember the coaching we did the other night?"

"Um. Yes." She remembered every ounce of trouble she'd gotten into with his "coaching." She remembered scaring herself half to death with how much she'd liked those reckless, wild kisses of his...and how shamefully much she'd liked being scared.

"Oysters are a bad food. A very, very bad food. We're talking a legendary aphrodisiac. Something about the chemistry puts sex on your mind. So if a guy kidnaps you for lunch, takes you to some deserted place, feeds you oysters..." Grave as a monk, Spence shook his head to illustrate this absolute no-no.

Her eyes danced. He'd taken her down this road before... and he made it so easy to play. "I need to watch out for those kinds of guys, huh?"

"You send them packing lickety-split," Spence affirmed. "And the motorcycle's another thing. You always need to look at a guy's wheels. You get around a guy into cycles, now... he likes speed, he likes risk, he likes taking chances. Those fellas may seem like fun, but where's the staying power?"

"I need to avoid them, too, huh?" When they got down to dessert, they discovered the key lime pie had suffered some squishing in the packing process. No matter. It still tasted like nectar, and they both leveled pieces without a single break in the teasing banter.

"Yup. All those guys are bad news. Take it from me. I excelled in being bad news in my younger days, so I know exactly the kind of guy you need to stay away from. I've done all his moves. And there's another thing you've got to watch out for." Spence pushed aside all their empty plates and stretched out.

"Yet another thing, oh sage one?" Chuckling, she stretched out, too, her stomach so full she couldn't believe it, and soaked in the warmth of the sleepy sun.

"Yeah...there's a lot of calculating, manipulative sons of guns out there. Maybe it wouldn't even look like you were being set up. A little reckless ride, butter you up with lunch..." Spence lifted the sleeve on his wrist, checked his watch. "You feel like you couldn't be safer with the guy when you know you both have to be home in twenty minutes. So you think, this is fun, what's the harm?"

"True, true, that's exactly what I'm thinking," Gwen admitted.

"But after lowering your defenses, tiger, that's exactly when that kind of guy moves in. Sneaky. Slow. Making you feel...risky. Making you feel just a little...dangerous. Remember what I told you about knocking the guy's block off last time?"

She remembered. If this was a test to see if she'd mastered the art of knocking a guy's block off, though, she seemed doomed to fail it. She just had no fears that Spence meant anything serious. Even the habit he'd picked up of calling her "tiger" was his way of gently teasing her for being a mouse. Even when he leaned over her, even when his head blocked the sun and all she could see were his dark, dark eyes...she knew a kiss was coming. But it just seemed a part of his natural, gentle teasing, nothing she needed to raise her defenses about....

And then his lips touched down. And if she had a defense in the universe, it seemed to skip town. She tasted key lime pie and his sun-warmed mouth. She'd

tasted him before, she'd kissed him before, yet the
sweet, heady electrical charge galloped in a race
through her blood like a surprise.

It wasn't *her*. She'd never been pulled into the drug
of a man this way. Kissing Ron had always been nice.
Very nice. This wasn't *nice*. This was scaring herself
and loving the feeling. This was the teetering, tumbling ride on a roller coaster of excitement—dizzying,
reckless, with her heartbeat capering crazy-wild with
longing. Keeping her head was no problem. She was
no innocent virgin to be led through the nose by her
hormones. It was just...the wonder...of discovering how terrifyingly rich wanting a man could be. Of
being kissed with savoring thoroughness, by a man
who knew how to treat a woman like an irresistible
treasure and didn't hold back letting her know it....

His lips tasted, clung, took. He made a sound, low
in his throat, making her feel powerful and
sexy...when Gwen never in her life had felt powerful
or sexy as a woman, couldn't even imagine stirring
such feelings in a man. Her heartbeat pitched and
caught. One of his hands moved to her fanny, cupping her, kneading, molding her intimately against his
thighs and him. His other hand moved slower, snail
slow, sidling from her spine to her ribs, up to claim
ownership of the swell of one breast.

A plain white T-shirt and a plain white bra trans-
formed—a mom of two boys transfigured. She was
satin and silk where he stroked and rubbed. She had
the figure of a young girl where he teased and trea-
sured. She felt...desired...and a stinging, singing
"yes" sang in her blood.

If there was danger, she wanted it. If there was risk,
she craved it with him. Crazy or not crazy, she wanted

these feelings, these moments with him, had the poignant and painful instinct that she'd missed this her whole life. Missed him.

Slowly he lifted his head and severed that wild mustang ride of a kiss. Slowly his hands strayed back to safe territory, to her throat, then pushed away a disheveled tangle of hair from her forehead. His face was grave with tension. And those deep, dark eyes focused intensely on hers.

"Gwen?" he murmured.

It didn't seem a very complex thing, to answer the simple call of her name. But her lungs temporarily couldn't seem to remember that tricky business about exhaling and inhaling. And her whole body still felt sensitized for his touch. And right then, she couldn't have guaranteed what her own name was...much less if she was willing to claim it being "Gwen."

"Did you hear what I was trying to tell you, brown eyes? It's just not safe to eat oysters. With anyone but me."

His voice was raw and hoarse and as tender as a secret.

She had to struggle to remember that he was teasing. She had to struggle to remember that she was a housewife and Spence lived in an entirely different world. She didn't believe he was playing with her, not in a harmful or hurtful sense. If they'd formed an unexpected bond, it had understandable roots—they lived so close; they understood each other's single-parenting problems, and they both seemed to be lonely. The building closeness she felt for him was real. Clearly he felt something for her, too.

The thing was keeping it in perspective. Kisses were one thing. Falling in love with him was another.

Spence was such an overwhelmingly potent package that he probably took his sexuality for every-day granted. It was just...she'd never taken electricity that powerful for granted. She'd never even known it was in her world.

"You teach unforgettable lessons, neighbor," she murmured, "about oysters."

"Hey, I was trying to teach you a lesson about being safe. About only taking risks with a guy you felt safe with."

His eyes seemed to hold some deep, serious message, but Gwen couldn't read it—or him. *Safe,* her mind echoed, thinking that he was a cyclone and an avalanche and a hurricane wrapped up in a single package. Thinking that he was her worst nightmare. Thinking that she'd never felt so reckless or so free or so wonderful in her life—as when she was with him. Even if she was begging for heartache.

"In fact, that's a lesson that goes both ways." Spence lurched to his feet. "Guess who's driving the Harley home?"

Her jaw dropped. "You're pointing your finger at me? Have you lost all your noodles? You think you'd be safe with *me* driving that monster machine?"

"Hey, I've been chased by more women than I can count. You think it's only women who get preyed on by manipulative, calculating predators? I don't give up my keys, not anymore, unless I feel safe with a woman."

"I'll kill us both," she announced.

"I don't think so."

"We both have children. Children dependent on us. We need to get home in one piece."

"And we will. You're dying to get your hands on the controls, admit it. You think I can't see that rampant lust in your eyes?"

Likely he did, drat the man. "Maybe there's a little desire. But that doesn't mean I'm suicidal," she said firmly.

He dangled the ignition key in front of her eyes. "Guts, Ms. Stanford. A few nights ago, you were miserable because you didn't think you had any. By the time you get us home, you'll know you do."

Seven

"Spence?"

Spence had just yanked on his suit jacket for the 10:00 a.m. staff meeting when Barbara flashed into his office.

"I just realized I had these files on my desk—thought you might need them for the meeting," she said.

"You're right..." Faster than an eyeblink, she handed him the manila folders. And with a skilled, subtle move, managed to accidentally brush her breast against his arm at the same time. Barbara Stuart was one of his finest up-and-coming account executives. She was also a maestro at those skilled, subtle moves. "Thanks," Spence said dryly.

"You have time for a drink after work?" she asked. "I'd really like the chance to discuss the Minson account with you privately."

It wasn't the first time he'd seen the implicit invitation in those radiant blue eyes. "I've got twenty minutes free right after this staff meeting. Come back to the office."

Barbara made a moue of disappointment. "That's no help. Your office is about as private and quiet as Grand Central Station."

Definitely true, Spence thought, but he'd chosen an office with inside windows—and an open-door policy—for a purpose. Visibility cut down on employees fretting or imagining what went on in the boss's inner sanctum. Half his staff were women. His choice, and he not only liked them, he valued them. Most were as good as Barbara, high-profile, competent, aggressive go-getters. The same personality ingredients that made them successful in marketing, though, could create an occasional sensitive problem. Barbara reminded him of his ex-wife. Man chasing had always been May's favorite contact sport.

Minutes later he strode into the staff room, greeting employees, grabbing a fresh hot mug of coffee, not thinking of the meeting ahead as he should...but of Gwen.

He couldn't imagine her chasing a man.

In his youth, no denying it, he'd loved being chased. A flash of leg had been enough to stir his hormones. Still did. But it had been a lot of years since he believed hormones and getting naked had anything to do with good sex—or a relationship worth having.

Brunner ambled in, then Kath and Seivers, but a couple of staff members were still missing. An upcoming project should have been on his mind. Successfully marketing anything in St. Augustine required bringing fresh ideas to old history. His concentration should have been on the brainstorming session ahead. Instead, waiting for the last employees to wander in, his mind strayed yet again...to the memory of Gwen's shrieks of laughter on the rented Harley. She was afraid she didn't have guts? She'd belted around curves at wind-whistling speeds, a daredevil sparkle in her eyes, color streaking her cheeks like red fire.

She not only had guts; she had an incredible zest and love for life, no matter what she was doing. She took such delight in kids. In messes. In sunny days and making brownies. In kisses at a picnic lunch, flavored with orange wine, kisses that leveled him like a knockout punch. Nothing, but nothing, was a hotter turn-on than honest emotion. And Gwen was power-packed honest, a concentrated package of rich, real emotion.

He wasn't just falling in love with her, Spence mused. He'd fallen. Like the Titanic trying to win against an iceberg. He knew the risks. He knew she was wary of getting involved with any man. But...

"Mr. McKenna?"

Jules snagged his attention, and abruptly he saw that the full staff had congregated now. Swiftly he started the meeting. Fifteen minutes later the elegant conference room resembled an imminent riot—by design. Spence ran his staff meetings like a free-for-all: loud voices as common as laughter, the flow of competing ideas encouraged; and no one shied from an argument.

Voices were heatedly raised in debate when Mrs. Raker suddenly stepped in and caught his eye. "You have a call," she mouthed.

His executive assistant would never have interrupted this kind of meeting unless there were an emergency—and an emergency meant a problem with April. Spence hustled to the closest phone in the next office.

The problem wasn't his daughter, but Gwen's son—Josh. Something had happened at school, and the child had been sent to the principal's office. He needed bailing out.

So much for upcoming, two-million-dollar projects. Spence canceled the staff meeting and hit the parking lot at a fast jog.

Gwen was locked up all day at the University of North Florida. This he knew because he'd set up the appointment for her. Although she was serious about seeking a new career, it wasn't as if she had a cut-and-dried goal in mind. He'd found a place that did testing to help her sort out what she wanted. She'd bought the idea, but where he had Mary Margaret as backup for April, she never left the house so far that her sons couldn't immediately reach her. She hadn't budged until he'd volunteered to be the school reachee.

Not for the first time, it struck him that it was a hell of a way to woo a woman. A guy was supposed to send roses. Not bully his lady into developing whole new interests that didn't remotely include him.

Spence felt like he was floundering in quicksand. He understood she needed independence. He also understood that a caged bird didn't sing . . . and that it was a man who'd caged her before. But she was so positive she wanted *reckless*. And he damn well loved that new and precarious reckless spirit of hers, but it seemed mighty unlikely he could win her trust by kidnapping her for a motorcycle ride.

Bailing her son out of hot water had more potential—assuming he didn't blow it.

Minutes later Spence barreled into the school office with a frown wedged on his forehead. He couldn't imagine what kind of trouble Josh could have waded into. His April and her Jacob were both mischief prone, but Gwen's seven-year-old was more of a studious little philosopher.

The school receptionist didn't keep him waiting, ushered him right into the principal's office. Mr. Bartholomew was a big, six-foot bear of a man, with one of those pumpkin faces that showed no wrinkles or age. Spence glanced at him and was further mystified. The principal certainly showed no sign of being angry or upset.

Josh sure did, though. The urchin was huddled in a chair, his tears not long dried, his skinny shoulders hunched up in utter misery.

"Hey, sport." Spence took the ally seat next to him and clutched a big hand on his nape. "So what's the deal here?"

It was a lo-o-o-ng story, which Mr. Bartholomew hadn't been able to get out of him completely... until now. Josh had been too upset to tell it. It seemed some kid in the second grade brought in a frog for science. Josh was into frogs. If you pet 'em a certain way, they spit out this wet stuff. There was some kid in the fourth grade who'd read something about girls; if you touched them in a certain spot, they got wet, too.

All they were doing was discussing this when Mrs. Merkel, the second-grade teacher, suddenly got all upset. She yelled at him about *where* did he hear that and not allowing that kind of talk in her classroom. Josh didn't get what put her liver in an uproar, but it wasn't hard to tell she was upset, and trying to be nice, he told her maybe it wasn't true of all girls and not to feel bad if she didn't get wet. Next thing, she's dragging him down the hall by the ear to the principal's office and parking him there. "Mrs. Merkel went back to the class, but she was mad. I mean really, *really* mad. She told me my mom was gonna wash my mouth out with soap."

Spence, by this time, had a hand over his mouth. Mr. Bartholomew was rubbing his eyes. Hard.

"Mom's gonna kill me, and I don't even know what I did. Mrs. Merkel says I owe the whole class an apology for talking dirty. I wasn't talking dirty. I was talking about frogs. I never said any of those words you're not supposed to say around girls. And Mrs. Merkel says I can't come back to class until my mom knows what I did."

When Spence met the principal's eyes, Mr. Bartholomew noisily cleared his throat. "It would seem we're dealing with a little misunderstanding here."

"Mountains and molehills come to mind," Spence concurred wryly. "If you don't mind a suggestion, I'm thinking that Josh has had a rough day, maybe best to just take him home. And that would give you a chance to catch Mrs. Merkel when she's free and um, explain the situation."

"Sounds like a plan to me." Mr. Bartholomew's eyes twinkled. "Although if you'd like to immediately talk to Mrs. Merkel yourself—"

"No, no. That job's all yours," Spence said magnanimously. "Let's hit it, Josh."

Josh, it seemed to Spence, needed a chocolate milk shake to recover from this trauma. The urchin was used to being the class ace. He'd never been in trouble before. He was down to the slurping depths of a two-scooper at the local Steak & Shake before some of the side ramifications seemed to occur to him. "Why would Mom wash my mouth out with soap?"

"Your mom isn't going to do that," Spence assured him.

He thought. "Mom says I come up with an awful lot of confounded stuff. But she says it's a good thing I'm curious and I should never stop asking questions. She never got mad at me before when I asked stuff."

"And she won't be mad at you now, sport."

"You sure?"

"Yup."

"I guess that girls don't have that wet spot like frogs, huh? Is that why Mrs. Merkel was so mad? Because she's not like a frog?"

"Um..." Spence paid for the shake and rapidly stood up. It was a hell of a strange time to discover he was falling as hard and hopelessly for the kid with the earnest face and the irrepressible cowlick as he'd already fallen for the mom. He was no good with these questions. So far April hadn't asked him anything too tricky. Nothing where he couldn't fall back on the handy Mr. Rogers line about boys being fancy on the outside and girls being fancy on the inside. "I think Mrs. Merkel was upset because she misunderstood what you were talking about. She thought you were trying to talk about sex, not frogs."

"Sex? What'd I say that had anything to do with sex?"

It only took a few minutes to drive home. Way too few. Not nearly enough time to stall or hope Josh would forget the question. "Well, I don't know exactly what that fourth-grader told you, but he may—*may*—have been referring to a biological response that happens to some adult women in, um, a love relationship."

"Huh? You mean women spit like frogs when they love somebody?"

Spence could feel sweat forming on his brow as he pulled into the driveway. *Gwen. Save Me.* How could he guess how she'd handle sex questions with a seven-year-old? Besides knowing damn well she'd do it better than him. "No. I just mean that grown women— and men—have certain biological responses when they love each other. Your mom would probably love to explain more about this. Actually, though, I think you'd find it pretty boring to hear about at seven . . . I mean, frog behavior is a lot more interesting."

"Girls are pretty boring," Josh affirmed, then quickly seemed to realize he could have offended Spence. "Except for April. She's okay. And Mom, of course. Do you like my mom?"

Mary Margaret, thank God, was home, and predictably charged out of the kitchen at the sound of a child's voice. No child Spence had ever met could resist MM's cookies and milk and after-school story telling.

It seemed Josh could. Not five minutes later, he tracked Spence down at the desk in the den. Possibly the urchin hadn't had a sitting-duck male adult around in a while, because he perched on the corner of the pecan desk like a pint-size Kierkegaard. "So . . . what do you think about the God thing?"

"Pardon?"

"You know. Where's God? Everybody seems to think they know. Is He everywhere? Is He in heaven? I mean, where do you think He *really* is, for Pete's sake?"

Spence pulled at his collar, thinking how those brown eyes tugged at him, thinking of sons. Thinking of stepfathers. Thinking that if he got any of these perilously difficult questions wrong, he could blow it with Gwen . . . and Josh.

April and Jacob popped home from school at the same time and tore through the house, tracking crumbs and noise and letting out after-school energy. Not Josh. Even his dullest answers didn't seem to budge Josh from the corner of his desk. It was after four before he heard Mary Margaret greeting Gwen at the front door and the women's voices pealing laughter. He heard her track down her youngest for a hug and a smacking hello.

Then she was there. In his doorway. Wearing cocoas and creams, a coral cameo at her throat, her hair ruffled from the wind. Josh rushed her. "Hey, Mom, I got in trouble for talking to Mrs. Merkel about frogs."

"Oh, yeah?" She showed no surprise, just ruffled his hair and stole a quick squeeze of a hug.

"She got sex confused with frogs. I think you better explain about sex to her."

"Okay." Again, Spence marveled. She didn't even bat an eye.

"Spence fixed everything. It's okay now."

"That was nice of Mr. McKenna to get you out of hock. Did you remember to thank him?"

"Sheesh, no. Thanks, Spence."

"You're welcome, sport." Josh took off—but thankfully his mom didn't. Her sudden grin was winsomely full of the devil.

"I'll bet you're ready for a whiskey straight. I know you've been exposed before, but when Josh really gets started with the questions, I feel like I've been through a mental marathon." Her grin died quickly then. "But I'm really sorry you had your workday interrupted because of a problem with one of mine—"

"Hey, you had a workday interrupted because of April not long ago. It felt good to return the favor, and your son was more fun than any workday, believe me. I'm pretty sure we covered sex, religion and politics in the first hour, then moved right into world philosophies and scientific technology."

She chuckled again. "That mind of his just doesn't stop. Is Mrs. Merkel going to survive whatever that little contretemps was about? I know she's a little on the buttoned-down side..."

Spence explained what happened. Watching her respond with both soothing calm and humor made him want to shake his head. Gwen persisted in seeing herself as some kind of weak mouse. He'd never seen it. Nothing a child did ever threw her. She never bucked a problem or a responsibility or anything tough. Maybe she didn't have a showy brand of assertiveness, but her strength was so clear to him, to everyone she touched. Gwen was the only one who didn't see it. "I almost forgot to ask...how did the day of testing go?"

Her face lit up with color and sparkle. "Splendiferous. Oh, Spence, I can't thank you enough for pushing me into trying those tests. The psychologist was wonderful. He gave me so many concrete ideas about jobs and work I could pursue. I brought home a dozen things to study..." She heard a shriek from the other room and immediately reached for her purse. "I'd better get my monsters home. We've stolen more

than enough of your time. But I owe you, Mc-
Kenna...."

She hustled toward him. Before he could guess what
she intended, she'd reached up and bussed his cheek.
It was nothing more than a casual, thank you, sisterly
smack. So swift. Spence caught the drift of some soft
feminine scent, a whisper of the texture of her, a flash
of something lightning bright with longing in her
eyes...and then she was gone. He heard her exuberantly herding her sons out the door and yelling something to Mary Margaret, but she was out of his sight—
and touching range—faster than an escape artist. That
kiss had been so brief that Spence's blood pressure had
time to rocket through the ceiling, but not time to
climb back down again. He dragged a hand through
his hair in frustration.

The only thing he'd seen Gwen run from yet was
him, and the building chemistry between them. Spence
understood her wariness and caution. He'd been there,
done that, bought the bumper sticker. She didn't want
to fall for anyone like her ex.

Only he kept hoping she'd see he was nothing like
Ron. He wanted her to see that he was crazy about her
boys. That he wasn't too bad with them. That in times
of trouble he was there for her...not holding her back
or caging her in, but making things possible.

So far, though, she hadn't seemed to notice any of
that. The only times she'd willingly been drawn to him
was when he played up to her hunger to be romanced,
to play, to indulge in an eensy bit of recklessness. And
since he damn well wanted to romance the woman,
there didn't have to be a problem.

But, Spence thought, there was. He didn't mind
going back to the ranch. He just couldn't shake the

uneasy, ominous feeling that that wasn't the real horse Gwen wanted to ride.

"Abby?" With the traveling phone tucked between her ear and shoulder, Gwen aimed for the closet. "I just called to ask your opinion—do you think gold earrings would go okay with the dress?"

Her sister's shriek nearly took out her eardrums. "You're finally wearing the dress? Who is he? And no—wear pearls."

"Okay. Pearls." Gwen burrowed in the closet and emerged with one shoe on and carrying the other. A glance at the bedside clock almost gave her a panic attack. Spence was due five minutes from now. She galloped to the jewelry case to find Paige's cameo and the pearl earrings. "Don't get your bees in a buzz. I'm just going out with my next-door neighbor. You think the dress is too fancy to wear to go out to dinner?"

"I think it's perfect for a nice dinner—now who is this guy?"

"He's a neighbor, I told you. A bachelor dad, the same way I'm a bachelor mom. It was Ron's night to take the boys, and Spence was free, and a couple days ago we were talking, laughing about dinnertimes with children. You know how kids are—the meat loaf had better not touch the peas, and they gag at casseroles, and they have a stroke if you put a sauce on anything. Anyway, it isn't a big deal, we just sort of decided it'd be fun to have a real, grown-ups-only dinner for a change—"

Her older sister interrupted this lengthy explanation with a most unladylike snort. "Quit trying to sell me bologna."

"There's no bologna." Gwen flipped the phone to the other ear to screw in the pearl earring. Then nearly stabbed her jugular when she attached the cameo pin to the throat of the dress.

"Who do you think you're talking to? Mom? This is *me*. You've turned down every guy who asked you out for the last two years. Paige and I have yelled at you up one side and down the other to go out again. Something's gotta be damned special about this guy to budge you."

"We're not 'going out.' It's not a 'date.' You've got this all wrong." Gwen pushed on the last shoe, then stepped back to get a look at herself in the mirror...and immediately felt a fearful, sinking sensation.

She looked all wrong. The ivory dress clung alluringly to her full breasts and draped in swirls over her hips. The texture was shivery, sexual. Sexy, but in a soft feminine way. The cameo at her throat set off the dress perfectly, but the dress belonged to the carefree, sensual woman in the cameo. Not to her.

She wasn't sexy. She wasn't carefree. She was the same-old, same-old, ever practical and responsible Gwen. Beneath the hectic color in her cheeks was still a cookie maker. Beneath the strapless bra was still a mouse...whose heartbeat was suddenly racing like a trapped animal's.

Abby, twenty-five hundred miles away in Los Angeles, picked up on her sudden silence with a sister's unerring intuition. "What's wrong? This guy's far more important to you than you're letting on, isn't he?"

"No. Heavens, no." Determinedly Gwen pivoted away from that image in the mirror. "Spence is in the mover-and-shaker circles. Nothing like me. It's just that we live so close that it's been handy to help each other out with our kids sometimes. He *is* a special friend, but he's kind of like, well, a...mentor." Memories of kisses sprang into her mind. Lethally unforgettable memories. Intimate memories, of kisses so rich and wild and tantalizing with promise that she was tempted to forget how hugely unalike they were. And suddenly her heart felt squeezed in an emotional vise. Her heart knew damn well she didn't see Spence as any "mentor."

"A mover and a shaker?" Abby's voice instantly turned protective. "Gwen, the only man you *have* to avoid is anyone like Ron. That jerk was just so forceful and demanding that he did his damnedest to swallow you up—"

"Spence is absolutely nothing like that. He's never demanded one thing from me." Yet abruptly, Gwen rubbed two fingers on her temples. Even to herself, she couldn't deny that Spence was a dynamite type who took charge.... She clearly remembered the way he'd railroaded her into the picnic, into driving the Harley, into that first kiss in her backyard that swept her off her feet. She saw him honestly. She knew precisely, exactly, why falling in love with him would be a dangerous mistake for her.

"Believe me, I'm smarter than I used to be," she told her sister. "I'd never fall again for someone where I didn't feel...equal."

"You're equal to anyone, you nitwit."

"Your sisterly bias is showing," Gwen teased with a chuckle. "I just meant that I need to feel I have something equal to offer in a relationship. Where I can hold my own. Feel strong on my own. And Spence—

he already knows I'm a mouse. In fact, that's partly what's made him such a special friend. I can be honest with him, knowing he isn't the least personally interested in me—''

In the distance she heard the peal of the front doorbell. And at the same time she caught the thudding sound of pounding on her back door. "Good grief, Ab, I have to go lickety-split. Catch you later."

Gwen hung up, grabbed her evening bag, and unsure which door to answer first, pelted on high heels for the front door because it was closer.

The door was already opening before she reached it. She was expecting Spence. She definitely wasn't expecting to see her blond, blue-eyed ex-husband poke his head around the door, dressed in an Italian tailored suit, looking, as ever, like a model for *GQ*.

One glimpse of his expression, though, and she could see Ron was ticked off. The door wasn't even half-open before Josh and Jacob swarmed past their dad, Josh wailing and crying and coughing up a storm.

Instinctively she bent down to scoop him close.

"Good thing you're here," Ron snapped. "I have a dinner party scheduled for tonight, for God's sake. I barely got the boys home before Josh started throwing up. I don't know what the hell's the matter with you, letting him go out when he's sick. Just because it was my custody time doesn't mean you couldn't show some common sense—''

Josh had had absolutely no symptoms of not feeling well earlier. Gwen would have explained, but there was no chance. Her first priority was checking out her son, feeling Josh's forehead and getting a good look at his eyes. Jacob was chattering ten for a dozen about some toy he'd left at Ron's house, and Josh was talking just as constantly.

"Mom, I feel awful *everywhere.* Even in my feet. Even in my head. I think I'm gonna die."

"I can't cope with a sick kid, not with a dinner party going on, and no big surprise, he started crying for you," Ron said, in clipped tones. "I can't believe you didn't know he was getting sick. I told you about the flu going around, told you what to watch for—"

Ron was still winding up when Josh tugged on her dress and informed her, "Mom, I think I'm gonna throw up again."

There was just no getting a rein on the pandemonium breaking loose. Ron was still ranting on, and Jacob was trying to talk to her, and she'd just scooped up Josh to race with him into the bathroom...when she heard an extremely sexy tenor clear his throat to announce his presence.

Spence had come in from the back door. Undoubtedly when no one had responded to his knock, he'd come seeking his dinner partner for the evening.

Gwen had a second and a half to notice he'd dressed up and looked to-die-for commanding. And another second and a half to feel that sinking sensation in her stomach again. She had to be crazy, plumb crazy, to fool herself into thinking a dress and a hairdo changed her into someone she wasn't.

There wasn't time to greet him. Josh needed her *now,* but even on the fast sprint down the hall to the bathroom with her son, she heard the telltale silence behind her as the two men confronted each other.

Assuming she survived the next few mortifying minutes, Gwen decided she was going to dig a hole in the St. Augustine beach and climb in. At that precise

moment she knew how secretly and fiercely she'd
wanted this romantic evening with Spence...and knew
how stupid she was to even dream of fairy-tale malar-
key when her real life was as far from fairy-tale as you
could get.

Eight

In the moonlit room, Gwen leaned down to kiss Josh and to tuck the blanket more snugly around his neck. The kiss was feather light. She didn't want to wake him. It was almost ten. She was pretty sure his stomach blues were over, because his cheek was cool, no sign of fever, and he'd been sleeping deeply for a couple hours now. Still, she left the bedroom door open in case he called her in the night.

Considering the hour, she should probably be peeling off the ivory silk dress and tumbling into bed herself. Instead she aimed for the kitchen, turned on the burner and rummaged in the cupboard for tea. Peppermint. Maybe that'd settle her nerves.

Waiting for the kettle to boil, she heard the fridge click on, the restless tick of the kitchen clock, the low drone of the TV she'd left on in the Florida room. It was amazing how loud a completely silent house could

be. Earlier, there'd been a strangely loud silence when
Spence had met her ex-husband, too.

The kettle whistled. Swiftly she poured the boiling
water into a china mug and dunked in the peppermint
bag. Spence had left quickly when he'd realized Josh
was sick, and to her, said nothing more about their
canceled dinner date, except not to worry, they could
do it another time. He'd had a few choice things to say
to her ex-husband, though.

Gwen sipped at the scalding tea, remembering the
confrontation between the two men. At the time she'd
been in the bathroom with Josh, with no possible way
to play peacemaker or referee. Neither role, of course,
was required. They were both grown men. But Ron,
positively, had never found another man in her house,
never seemed to expect there would be anyone but him
in her life. And Spence could surely have found some
man-to-man way of establishing that he was only a
neighbor and friend—but he hadn't even tried to do
that. Instead, he'd taken Ron on.

She hadn't seen the men, had missed whole slices of
their conversation...but she'd heard enough. Their
exchange of greetings had been innocuous enough.
But then Spence said something like, "Knowing
Gwen, no matter what she'd planned for an evening,
she would have canceled if she knew one of the boys
were sick. But I could have sworn she mentioned that
you were a doctor?"

And Ron, ever establishing territory, had swiftly
asserted that he was.

Spence's voice had echoed surprise. "I'd think, being a doctor, that you'd be pretty comfortable handling a sick child. Especially rather than making the

choice of dragging him in a car all over town to bring him back here again.''

Ron had bristled up faster than a defensive porcupine. ''The point is that Gwen never even told me Josh was sick—''

''I understand,'' Spence had said smoothly. ''I'm a single dad myself, so I know how easy it is to panic over a sick child. And even if I had multiple doctoring degrees, I'd still probably run to Gwen, too. She's just incredible at handling the tough stuff like this, isn't she?''

When Gwen finally emerged from the bathroom with Josh, the two men were still standing in the hall— but Spence was in the process of shuttling her ex-husband out the door. ''Don't worry about a thing— we'll take it from here. I know you're in a hurry to get back to your dinner party. Real nice to meet you, hope to see you again sometime—''

And then, woosh. Not a slam. But Spence definitely and firmly closed the door in her ex-husband's extremely startled face. Gwen couldn't help shaking her head. ''Good grief, how'd you *do* that?''

''How'd I do what?'' Spence asked.

''Make him disappear,'' she said dryly.

''Ah, well. I had a run-in with a bully when I was in fourth grade. Discovered something interesting. No bully has an interest in a fair fight. If they can't sucker you into being intimidated and kowtowing, it's just no fun to pick on you, and the bully invariably backs down.''

Josh was still sick, and Jacob was clamoring for her attention, and Spence left too quickly for her to say anything else to him. But everything about the confrontation between the two men lingered in her mind.

Spence had more than defended her. He'd somehow turned Ron's tirade of blaming her into something else entirely.

Normally—okay, *always*—Gwen tended to defend her ex-husband. Partly because she never wanted to put down the boys' dad in front of them, and partly because of pride. It bit, that others would think she had the poor judgment to marry a creep. Ron had ambition and dedication and could be downright charismatic—darn it, there were always real, solid reasons why she'd been drawn to him.

But he'd always put her down, Gwen mused. He'd always liked her kowtowing, always found a way to make her miserable if she disagreed with him, and aimed straight for her vulnerable spots when he wanted something. That bully streak had always been there. She'd just never considered that "bully" tag until Spence had called a spade a spade.

She had never seen a way to cope with it, either— until now. A couple weeks before, she recalled telling Spence that she wished she could take an assertiveness course to deal with her ex. Whether or not he intended it, he'd given her one for free. Spence hadn't tolerated her being put down for two seconds. Just maybe, she didn't have to, either.

Abruptly she realized that her teacup was empty. Definitely time for bed. Yet after she checked on the boys and turned out the lights, she found herself back in the kitchen doorway.

Sleepiness just wouldn't come. It was a black velvet night, a dreamer's night, with a wand of stars sprinkling the sky and just the hint of a silky breeze. The three-quarters moon was a smoky, moody silver, perfect for spinning fantasies. Dew sparkled in the grass like magic crystals.

From across the yard, she caught a glimpse of white, and for a moment couldn't fathom what it was. The flash of white moved toward her, across one lawn, to her fence and then past the gate. By that time she recognized the white was a man's shirt, could see it was Spence...and her heart was suddenly racing, dipping and pitching like a catamaran in a high wind.

"You still up, neighbor? How's our boy doing?"

She smiled. "I just looked in on him a couple minutes ago. He's sleeping like a log."

"You think it's a flu?"

"There's no fever. Too soon to tell yet, but I think he just had a rotten tummy upset." She wasn't sure what he was doing here. She was even less sure where the sudden, fierce longing came from, but it was like a devil in her blood, a quickening just because he was here, near, close enough to feel brushed and touched by those deep, dark, sexy eyes. "I'm really sorry I had to cancel our dinner."

"No reason to apologize. Kids come first. But I can see you're still dressed."

It felt silly, now, not to have changed out of the ivory silk dress earlier. For a while she'd been legitimately too busy, caretaking Josh, making dinner, cleaning up and just doing "mom" things. After that...well, maybe she'd kept it on from sheer stubbornness. Who knew if she'd ever have a chance to wear the dress again? And the texture of the silk against her skin made her feel feminine and sensual and just...different. Good different. "You got too busy to change, too, I see."

His suit jacket was gone, but the moonlight clearly illuminated the starched white linen shirt, the tie, the navy blue dress pants. "Not too busy. I just happened to think about how you got royally cheated tonight," Spence said.

"Cheated?"

"Yeah. Canceling the grown-ups-only dinner couldn't matter less. We can do that anytime. But I noticed that moon earlier. It was on your list of reckless things you wanted to do, wasn't it? Dance in the moonlight?"

She was startled that he'd remembered, then embarrassed. "That silly list. Honestly, I keep telling you, I never really meant—"

Spence didn't seem to hear her. "It's a cinch you're not going anywhere out of earshot from Josh tonight. But it's only ten. It's an unbeatable moon. No one seems to be up in the entire neighborhood but us, and something tells me you have a radio or tape deck somewhere in the house."

"You're teasing," she announced.

But he wasn't.

Spence could see she thought the whole idea was foolishness, and regretfully she had time to build up more nerves. He found a portable radio in her kitchen to bring outside, but tuning it to something livable took a while. Boisterous rock and roll could have wakened the neighbors.

He definitely didn't want to wake any neighbors.

He wanted slow music. Real, real slow. So slow it wouldn't wake anyone...but her. Eventually he discovered a station playing some old R & B, and then captured her cold, nervous hands and pulled her onto the grass. "I've never done it, either. Danced by moonlight. You're gonna have to help me."

"I was thinking about helping you by discreetly calling 911. If anyone catches us doing this—"

"No one's going to catch us." A rash promise, Spence knew, but in the dark shadows off her patio, her eyes were brighter than quicksilver.

Maybe she felt foolish; maybe those slim, damp hands he pulled around his neck were cold with nerves, but there was excitement in those eyes. The night air carried the spices of flowers and grass and sea breezes, and the radio had the kindness to play something old and hokey and unbeatably corny...but even so, a true romantic atmosphere was tough to pull off. The lawn was dew-soaked and ticklish. Swing sets were in sight. Mr. Williams let out his cat across the far courtyard.

She was stiff...until he tried a Valentino dip. She started giggling then, a real giggle, a Gwen giggle. Her chuckling faded, though, when he pulled her snug in his arms, tucking her head between his chin and shoulder. Her heart beat against his like slow, heavy thunder. The radio switched to a crooning love song so old he couldn't name it, couldn't dance to it, either. But then, he wasn't trying to dance to the song. He was trying to dance to Gwen.

Earlier, he'd been tempted to rip out her ex's heart. Tonight was the first time he'd had a mirror view of how the jerk crushed her. Like any bully, Ron attacked where she was most vulnerable—her kids—and in front of an audience where she'd be least able to defend herself. That he just showed up, no call ahead, expecting Gwen to instantly jump for any change in his plans, gave Spence a clear picture of how living with

him must have been—and how a long-term effect on
her self-confidence had happened.

Even more now, he understood her need for freedom—her need to feel self-sufficient, under no one's
thumb.

But right now, he thought she needed to play. She
was damned outstanding at carefree play around the
kids, had an indomitable spirit of fun given freely to
everyone around her...but that wasn't play for *her*.
Spence had in mind a more dangerous kind of fun. A
totally distracting brand. More naughty. More wicked.
He swirled her around the yard, cuddling her breasts
against him tightly. He teased Gwen with electricity,
letting the moonlight wash a little magic dust and the
music spin them breathless. And when she was hopelessly out of breath, he hauled her close again, hip to
hip close, barely shuffling, the beat of the music
echoing other, more primal rhythms.

Mating rhythms seemed impaled in his brain. He
wanted to kiss her. Needed to. But he needed and
wanted more than kisses from Gwen, and he was
afraid to start, wary that he couldn't guarantee a
functioning brake pedal if he started anything with her
again. Because Josh had been sick, Spence strongly
suspected she'd never have her mind completely off
her son tonight. He knew her and he understood. But
the next time he kissed her, he wanted her full, undis-
tracted attention.

God knew, she'd captured his.

The music suddenly stopped. An announcer sleepily announced the hour of eleven and some fine deal
for a used car. She lifted her head, looked at him.
Spence would have bet a month's salary that she'd
never heard that fine, used-car deal. There were more

stars in her eyes than the whole damn sky. Desire had painted her face with a soft brush. The same longing was reflected in the warmth of her body, the yielding way she molded to him.

"What are you doing to me, McKenna?" she whispered helplessly.

"The same thing you're doing to me. With me." He stepped back. Touched her cheek. He was afraid to say too much, afraid to scare her away. "Maybe you think you need a coach, tiger. But everything we're doing together is just as new to me. And I'll tell you what I feel. My whole world burns brighter when we're together. I think you have magic in you."

"No," she denied.

"Yeah, you do."

Three afternoons later, Gwen was still thinking about that night. Spence had left so swiftly. Just like that. The flash of his white shirt moved across the yard and disappeared into the darkness... like a pirate sneaking in, sneaking out. Or like a romantic rogue, a thief of hearts, come to visit long enough to turn her on, turn her upside down, turn her mind and body into butter... and then gone, making her wonder if she'd imagined it. Making her think that the fantasy had been so rich and wild that she'd have to be nuts to think it was real.

Spence had wanted her, though. His body had told her that explicitly and unmistakably.

And the wayward thought kept dawdling through her mind that she had a choice. She could be a good girl, the way she'd always been—a serious, sane, responsible, always-trying-to-please-and-do-her-best good girl—and ignore the desire between them. Or she could be an idiotic damn fool and...well...*do* something about it.

"Mom?" Jacob tugged on her shoulder.

"What, honey?" Gwen didn't lift her head from the puddle of spilled grape juice she was wiping off the floor. She wasn't exactly sure how seven kids ended up at her house after school. One of the neighboring moms had the flu. Her kids had popped over and somehow more kids had reproduced from there.

"Mom, could I have a black mamba?"

"Not today, sweetheart."

"They're the fastest snakes on the whole planet. And they grow to be a zillion feet long. And they'll kill you so fast you can't believe it, because they are really, really poisonous. I mean, they're awesome. We need one, Mom."

"It sure sounds like it. Although it might be just a little tricky to have a black mamba as a house pet, don't you think?" Gwen carried the soaked rag into the living room, stopped, wondered what the sam hill she was doing anywhere near the living room, and retracked to the kitchen. Her brain just seemed to be functioning at a penny short of a cent. Seven kids galloping around, the TV on, the kids' computer on, the kitchen table strewn with drying finger paint artwork, and That Man was still managing to distract her.

Jacob trailed in her wake. "I got an answer for that. We just gotta get a secretary bird at the same time we get the black mamba."

"This solves the problem, huh?"

"Yup. See, black mambas don't have many pred'tors because they're so powerful and gruesome. But the secretary bird is one of them. They eat mambas. After they stomp 'em to death. So, all you gotta do to keep a mamba in line is get a secretary bird. And wouldn't you like to see a secretary bird stomp a black mamba to death?'' Her six-year-old stomp, stomp, stomped around the kitchen to illustrate said desired behavior.

"Gosh, I sure would. And I have to tell you, I'm so impressed with all this stuff you learned. I wouldn't have known one thing about black mambas if you hadn't educated me."

"You should know this stuff, Mom. Sheesh. You probably didn't r'lize that black mambas lived in Africa, did you?"

"Nope. I was ignorant about that, too. Boy, am I glad you're willing to tell me these things."

Someone pitched a bloodcurdling scream. Somewhere she heard water running—which was always an ominous clue that disaster was imminent. And somehow she found herself staring out the window at Spence's house, the soaked rag still dangling in her hand, thinking not about African mamba snakes but tigers.

He kept calling her tiger. If he'd called her honey in that same low, throaty tenor, she'd probably work up an ulcer fretting what the endearment meant. But except for what his voice did to her heartbeat, tiger didn't seem dangerous. She was pretty sure he meant it as a joke. A gentle way of teasing her for being a self-avowed, card-carrying, ace-pro mouse.

She wasn't a tiger. But she didn't seem to quite fit the mouse label anymore, either. Somehow over the last few weeks, she'd become a terrible person. And it had happened so easily. One day she'd been fantastic at guilt, outstanding at suffering, could have had a master's degree at being good. It seemed overnight she'd become selfish.

She liked feeling reckless, the way Spence made her feel reckless. She wanted to feel desired, wanted, the way no one but Spence had ever made her feel desired. She hadn't plumb lost her marbles. Her sons mattered far too much for her to ever adopt a "living for today" philosophy. But the nasty, wicked, irrepressible thought kept whispering through her mind that the children would never know what they never saw. She was old enough to have an affair. Old enough to make a mistake. Old enough to fall, insanely, miserably, dangerously in love if she damn well wanted to.

Gwen stared out the window until her vision blurred, and then squeezed her eyes closed tight. Who was she kidding? She was already in love with him. Hard. Stupidly. Irrationally. No two people could be more of an unmatched set. Long-term, Spence couldn't possibly be interested in a plain old homemaker. And she had a terrible track record at holding her own with a dynamo.

Put a black mamba and a secretary bird together, and as her son had helpfully pointed out, somebody was gonna get hurt.

What happened, though, if it were just her? If no one got hurt but her? If she had the guts, just once, to be like the woman in the cameo—carefree, open, with the courage and the spirit to embrace every experience life had to offer? Would it be so selfish if she just let something happen? With him. Only with him.

No man had ever moved her like Spence. No matter what the future held, she was painfully afraid she could regret it for the rest of her life if she threw away the choice, the chance, to know him as a lover.

Something splatted against her head. Instantly she felt the cold dribble of liquid down her neck. She whirled around . . . to find seven pairs of devil eyes— all pint-size—attached to extremely hopeful faces and mad giggling. And all, drat them, were holding water balloons.

Using her meanest and most authoritative voice, she roared, "Outside, you monsters!"

They giggled harder.

Well, hell. She gave chase, thinking where the pa-tooties was her mind? She knew about kids. She knew zip about seduction. And given all the children and busy schedules of their lives, she suspected there was a thousand to one chance she'd ever have the chance to seduce him, anyway.

She was safe. The way she'd always been safe.

And then the telephone rang.

Nine

An hour after the phone call from Spence, he hustled in her back door. "Got it. Extra large. Triple cheese. Mushrooms on half, no anchovies, should be enough extra-hot peppers to burn our throats for the next five, six hours."

Gwen chuckled. "I can smell it from here. Bring it in, bring it in. And you get hero status for life for thinking of this."

"Hey, all I did was suggest the pizza. It was Loretta and Stan who volunteered to take all the kids to the movies. With guts like that, who needs courage? You want the pizza on the table?"

"The table'll do fine. Just sit down and relax. I'll be there in two shakes."

Well, she meant to be. Spence had called with the impromptu pizza idea only a few seconds after Loretta telephoned about herding up the neighborhood kids for fast-food burgers and a movie. She'd bustled the boys into fresh clothes and a face-and-hands wash before letting them loose in public. There'd been no time—or reason—to change from the white shorts and plain raspberry T-shirt she was wearing. No time or reason for her to fuss in any way for such a casual shared dinner.

Yet she suddenly found herself hiking around the kitchen at the speed of sound. Cracking ice cubes, rummaging around for her good glasses, pouring iced tea, automatically adding a fresh sprig of mint to make the tea just a little fancier. Then the kitchen table looked so naked that she whisked around and found table mats. Then she foraged in the cupboard for company napkins instead of those on-sale easy-shred jobs she used every day. Then...

"Hey, tiger. Come and sit down before it gets cold."

She promptly sat down. Then bounced up again. They needed a spatula and a sharp knife. And maybe she was used to treating pizza as a finger food, but Spence might prefer real live silverware. And the flower centerpiece was right in his way...

"Um, Gwen? I know appearances are deceiving, but I swear I'm not helpless. If I need anything, I can get it myself. And I'll have to shoot you if you keep trying to wait on me."

She chuckled at his teasing threat...and sat. But the thought hit her with the subtlety of a blow from a blast furnace—she *had* been waiting on Spence, when she'd sworn from here to Poughkeepsie that she'd never catch herself waiting on another man again.

Tarnation, every other woman in the nineties seemed to drop the old traditional female roles with no sweat. She seemed the only one left with the problem.

Blast it, nurturing had always come naturally to her. Taking care of people just seemed to be a hopeless flaw in her nature. She didn't *mean* to. She was trying desperately hard to master this selfishness business. But it seemed an unnerving measure of how deeply she'd come to care for Spence that fussing over him was such a pleasure she'd forgotten it was an old, rotten habit she was trying to break.

Spence forked over a wedge of pizza on her plate big enough for a Marine, but he eyed her over the box top. "Are we, uh, nervous for some reason? Is something bothering you?"

"Heavens, no. Any night I don't have to cook is manna from heaven—I couldn't be more relaxed than a lazy slug on vacation."

"Lazy slug, huh?"

The skeptic appeared to need proof. She bit into a huge cheese-dripping chunk of pizza to illustrate how unnervous she was. Mutual starvation took over then. They both dove into the pizza like piranhas. Conversation shuttled from kids to St. Augustine politics to school to books. He liked history and an occasional thick saga. She liked romance and an occasional gruesome horror. Talking with him came so naturally and easily that the word *safe* sneaked into her brain. Maybe her feelings for Spence spiraled into the dangerous realm, but he'd always had the gift for putting her at ease and making her feel comfortable and safe with him.

Yet that word *safe* had been hanging out in her mind like an imbedded sliver for days. Safe was dull. Safe was predictable. Her whole life, she'd chosen the safe, traditional, foolproof woman roles, and she'd come damn close to boring herself to death.

A few minutes later Spence threw up his hands. "I see there're two pieces of pizza left, but I'm pleading mercy. How about you?"

"Definitely stuffed... but they sure weren't stingy with those hot peppers. I need another glass of iced tea, would you like one, too?"

"Sounds great—but I'll get it for both of us."

Spence sprang up to take their glasses to the pitcher by the sink. At the same time she moved to refrigerate the leftover pizza and toss out their paper plates.

He said something to her, but she didn't catch it.

She couldn't exactly explain what went wrong at that instant. Nothing was suddenly different. Her pulse was tumbling and pitching, but her sexual awareness of Spence was becoming as familiar as the sun rising. Her hormones had been in a tizzy since he walked in the door. That was old news. While they were both moving around the kitchen, his gaze skimmed the length of her, the bare legs, the pouchy T-shirt, the fresh sun-swept color in her cheeks. But it wasn't the first time he'd looked at her. It wasn't the first time those dark eyes of his lingered.

Maybe the clock ticked too loud. Maybe a door slammed somewhere. Positively there was no sane reason for her to suddenly whirl around and charge straight toward him.

He was half-turned, a sponge in his hand, so he had to see her catapulting toward him. He dropped the sponge. As if a completely insane woman had taken charge of her body, she surged up on tiptoe, her arms flew around his neck, and her lips crashed on his with the awkwardness of a fender-bender collision.

Shock rippled through her. At no time in her life had she ever completely abandoned her common sense. It was the first Gwen knew she even had the capacity to behave so appallingly.

Spence didn't seem to be suffering from the same appalled shock. He didn't even seem surprised. He kissed her back like he'd been waiting, pounce ready, for any excuse to get his hands on her. She'd never expected rewards for such rash, shameless behavior... but, oh God, there were.

He tasted like hot, hot peppers and cool ice. He tasted like everything she'd ever been afraid of. It was as if this hunger had been buried forever and was suddenly bubbling up to the surface with shivering speed.

He murmured something gentling, soothing, but she wasn't gentled, had no hope of feeling soothed. Braced against the sink edge, he drew her into the vee between his thighs. His mouth rubbed against hers, roughly, deeply, taking her tongue and offering his own right back. His thighs pressed so evocatively against her that she could feel the building beat and heat of his arousal. There wasn't a prayer of a chance that she could remember to be ashamed, not a prayer that she could keep anything on her mind... but those thighs. And that mouth. And the unmistakable evidence that he wanted her.

When he lifted his head, his eyes seemed darker than pewter and mesmerizingly intense. Dusty sunlight filtered through the kitchen window. Dusk was falling fast, but it was still daylight. In her kitchen. It was not the time or place for this to happen, for anything to happen, yet his gaze so fiercely searched her face. He didn't seem to notice anything about anything—but her.

"You'd better tell me what you want, tiger. Real clear, and real fast, because I'm not going to ignore that invitation in your eyes unless you tell me otherwise."

She couldn't think. She just wasn't prepared. On the back of her tongue she tasted risk, as dangerous and precarious as she'd ever faced before. "I...don't know."

"Yeah. I think you do."

"I..." Yeah, she knew what she wanted. She'd known for weeks. But so far the desire springing up between them had been accidental, incidental. It had never occurred to her that Spence would follow through. It had never occurred that he would want to, that he really wanted...her. Anticipation sluiced through her veins in a rush. But so did anxiety. "I'm not very good at throwing caution to the winds."

"Is that what you're thinking about doing, throwing caution to the winds?"

"Maybe." Words tumbled out. "Maybe yes. But the children are due home around nine, and I don't have any—"

"It's still two long hours before nine, and I have protection. I wasn't asking you a question about the details, tiger, I was asking you the big cheese question."

"How about a qualified yes?"

"What's the qualifying factor?"

"I'm scared."

"Sheesh. That's the toughest problem you can come up with?"

"Spence, it's a pretty damn big qualifying factor."

Apparently not to him. Apparently expressing a little vulnerable insecurity to Spence was like adding fuel

to a fire, a dash of gasoline, a splash of an ignitable
explosive.

He skimmed her raspberry T-shirt over her head,
tossed it. Then he kissed her; an embrace that certainly started in the kitchen but seemed to travel at its
own speed with a radar sense for where it wanted to
end up. His sweatshirt had disappeared by the time
they reached her bedroom door, and her bra had
somehow taken off somewhere.

So had she.

His lips washed a trail down her neck and throat.
Hands tugged at her white shorts, skidded, skimming
them off her. His mouth skidded, too, skimming the
cream off kiss after kiss. A damp palm cupped her
breast, kneaded it reverently, and then he dipped down
for a kiss that tongued the tip and left it tight and
burning.

Her knees wanted to buckle. As if Spence knew, he
yanked at the yellow-and-white comforter and stripped
the bedding down to bare, spare cotton. Then he leveled her on the cool, lemon sheets and kissed her
senseless, kissed her until there seemed nothing but
this liquid fire in her belly and a desire for him claw-
ing all through her.

He scraped away his pants, the last of his clothes,
everything separating them. She kept expecting inhibitions to show up, fears of being inadequate, not
enough woman, not skilled enough to please him.
She'd always known Spence's world had to be popu-
lated with women more sophisticated, more life-and-
sex experienced, than her. Those fears were real. They
just never seemed to have a chance to take hold.

She *knew* Spence. He had poise, confidence, was
always a hopelessly aggressive, take-charge dynamo.

Only not now. Not here. Not with her. Sunset gradually softened the room with deepening, darkening mauve shadows. That pale silvery dusk caught the side of his face, the deep river of emotion in his eyes. It changed things, when she discovered his hands were less than steady, his heartbeat was frantic as her own, that he was vulnerable ... no different from her.

The need pouring off him was naked, raw, lonesome. She'd sensed he was lonely, sensed he needed someone...but not her. She'd never really believed he could be out of control with her, for her, just for her. His pulse slammed each time she touched him. His breathing roughened like gravel. She stroked his smooth hot chest, the taut muscles, the long hard body, inhaling his textures, his scents, the flash-fire urgency of his response to her.

Maybe she wasn't sure of him. Maybe she doubted even trying to believe in a future between them. But loving him ... there was no doubt in her heart about that. She wanted him to be loved. She wanted him to *feel* loved, by her, and that compelling emotion drove her like nothing else ever had.

Wicked used to be one of the forbidden words in her vocabulary, along with *greedy* and *selfish*. But Spence seemed to see making love as a no-rules, no-holds-barred war...and tempted her to do the same. The battle began, a skirmish to see who could give more, a war for who could please whom first, an earthy, drugging-sweet battle to see who could tease and tempt the other beyond mercy.

At least until he ran out of patience. He'd lost his pants. Neither of them were sure when, and neither would have particularly given a royal banana where, except that he had protection in a pocket. Comforter, sheets, pillows flew in his hoarse, swearing search for his rumpled dockers. Both of them started laughing, but when he finally found the blasted packet, their smiles faded. Neither wanted any more distractions.

He hauled her beneath him in the tangle of sheets. His heartbeat as thrumming-hard as a drum. His arousal pressed insistently, intimately, between her thighs. He took a kiss that stole every last ounce of oxygen from her lungs, then took another.

"I love you, Gwen."

His voice was a whisper, fierce, almost angry with frustration. She heard what he said, believed he meant it. For now. She sieved her hands through his hair and answered him with an open-mouthed kiss, thinking that now was all that mattered. If she was begging for heartache later, she couldn't care. Nothing in her life had ever felt as right as loving him.

He tested first with his fingers and palm, stroking, coaxing, praising her in murmurs for being so ready for him. She was more than ready. She wanted him like fever and fire, and restlessly pushed against him to end such play.

Wrapping her legs tightly around him, she felt him plunge into her, filling that aching hollow. Her eyes squeezed shut and her senses turned knife sharp, every sight, sound, taste and texture acutely linked to him. Love was a gift, not a price. It was hers to give. Expressing love was the one thing that had always come naturally to her, but it was as if she'd been rehearsing her whole life for the one man who'd cherish the gift instead of using her for it. "Come to me," she whispered. "Come to me. Now, Spence..."

He began a driving rhythm to match her need, her fears, the wild racing love song in her heartbeat. They spun and rocked on the tangled sheets, climbing higher, then in a burst of fire and friction, soared free.

A sudden fretful wind ruffled the curtains. Clouds were roiling in a storm, but it wasn't here yet. The breezes sifted the vanilla and jasmine scents from the bedside bowl of potpourri. The room was fuzzy dark. Beneath the sheet, Spence's arms were still wrapped snugly around her.

Any second now Gwen expected to stop feeling...free. For weeks now she'd been on a self-reliance discovery mission. She wanted to be more free, but freedom was nothing she knew as an emotion before. Like the fairy tale about the caged bird who was too sad to sing, she didn't know it would feel like such a freeing of mind and spirit to have those cage doors opened . . . not that she wanted to scare Spence witless by breaking out in song.

He shared the same pillow. He was awake, his eyes on her face as cuddling warm as his arms draped around her. Desire curled through her when his hand strayed down in a lambent, stroking caress. When a woman felt as boneless as Silly Putty, it was hard to imagine that it was even possible to feel desire. Not again. And for sure, not this soon.

"Anyone ever tell you that your mouth is a miracle of nature?" Spence murmured. His fingertip traced her lower lip.

"Umm, no."

"How about your fanny? Were you aware that you have the most delectable, inspiring and enticing behind anywhere on the planet?" His palm managed to locate that body part, too.

"Uh, no."

"You took me out, tiger."

If she were feeling more like her sensible, practical self, she undoubtedly wouldn't have been tempted to believe him. Even in the dusty shadows, though, he looked wonderfully wasted. His hair was disheveled, his eyes drugged with softness. The harsh lines of tension and frustration carved in his expression were definitely gone now, and his voice was thicker than syrup.

She brushed a lock of hair from his brow, hungering to give back the huge riches he'd given her. "You more than took me out, McKenna. You gave me something back that I didn't even know I'd lost."

His eyebrows arched in question. "Explain? What did you think you'd lost?"

She hesitated. "I'll tell you. I want to tell you. But first, I don't want you worrying that our making love implies any noose around your neck or any obligation..."

Spence reached up and switched on the bedside lamp. The abrupt glow of soft yellow light made her eyes blink sleepily, yet he seemed suddenly wide awake, his gaze watchful on her face. "Were you afraid I'd bring up a terrifying word like *rings?*" When she didn't immediately answer, he said carefully, "I know you value your freedom."

"I'm trying to. Learning to. And it would really trouble me if you thought I'd suddenly become...dependent...because we made love." She'd been honest with him about the kind of unhealthy dependent relationship she'd had with Ron. She meant to reassure Spence that she would never let that happen with him. Yet the hand trailing her back suddenly stilled and tensed.

"You're no clinging vine with me, never have been, Gwen. But let's go back to the question we started with. What were you afraid that you'd lost?"

"Well, this is a little embarrassing to tell you..." That fretful breeze ruffled the curtains again. "But I was afraid of making love. Maybe ever again. The thing was, I used to feel pretty comfortable with sexual feelings. Not like I was any wild femme fatale or anything silly like that, but I had no particular reason to worry that I was inadequate or lacking...."

Her voice trailed off. As much as she was willing to be honest, somehow this was a ton harder to say than she'd expected.

Spence coaxed gently, "Just tell me."

"It was just...my marriage seemed to end the split instant I was no longer...useful. I never resented supporting my ex through medical school. But Ron practically hit a divorce lawyer at the speed of light when he finally set himself up financially with his practice. Until then, I didn't realize that my 'usefulness' was the only thing holding us together."

"Useful," Spence echoed the word.

"It preyed on my mind for the last couple years. That I could have been so naive as to think this part of our lives was okay, when he obviously wanted someone more...exciting. And yes, all that's over now. But I'd built up a fear of ever doing this again. With anyone. I was scared that I'd lost those feelings, scared I'd never been any good at it, scared I'd never just be able to...let go."

"Gwen—"

"No, just let me say it and finish it real quick." Her eyes had been darting all over the room, everywhere, anywhere, but on him. But she looked at him now and touched his cheek. "I felt more than free with you. I felt wonder, like an explosion. More than I knew I could feel. You gave me more than you know, McKenna, more than I can seem to tell you—"

He made a sound. Not loud, but sort of a husky growl from the back of his throat. Startling her even more, he abruptly scooped her beneath him and kissed her with the sizzling pressure of a brand. "We need to get a couple of things straight, tiger. Right now."

"We do, huh?"

"You're about to get a lecture on how exciting you are. How exciting I find you. And there's going to be a test on this later, so you better pay attention."

"I...um...yes, sir."

"I want it very, very clear that I don't think of you as *useful*. What you do to me is upsetting. Unsettling. Risky. And damned unnerving for a man who is never in the habit of losing control and doesn't have a clue how you manage to do it. Does that sound like I find you *useful*?"

"Umm, no." Apparently that was the answer he wanted to hear, because it earned her another kiss. This one in vivid color, bruise red and wet and blurring at the edges, melting into another kiss before either of them remembered to breathe in between.

"You're a lot of trouble, Ms. Stanford. I love your brand of trouble. If you—*damn*."

Like the cut in a film, his hand stopped, his mouth stopped, a halfway-to-another kiss stopped. His eyes shot to the bedside clock, then back to her face. He swallowed, thick and hard. "Gwen, it's ten to nine."

Her eyes shot wide then, too. "Holy horse feathers."

"The kids are all due back from the movies—"

"I know, I know. And you can't have April coming home to an empty house. And the boys—neither of us is dressed."

Both of them quit talking and hustled, fast. Spence hopped around the room as quickly as she did, scrambling into clothes and shoes, finding brushes, sweeping the covers back on the bed. A swift, hard kiss from him, a "we're nowhere near done with this conversation, tiger" and then he was bolting out the door.

A chuckle of laughter bubbled in her throat for a minute. Both of them had been running around like teenagers, scared of getting caught.

The thought of the children catching them sobered her quickly, though. She was a single mom. A twenty-four-hours-a-day ever-present and always-available single mom. Sneaking around her boys for an affair would never work. And her sons already counted on Spence in their lives, the same way April seemed to have become naturally attached to her.

I don't regret one minute we spent together, she thought fiercely. But a sudden clap of thunder made her jump. Lights flickered. Roiling clouds burst open in a pelting, noisy thunderstorm. She was waiting at the front door when Josh and Jacob raced into the house, heads wet from the sudden deluge, talking ten for a dozen about the movie they'd seen.

So quickly she was Mom again, not lover. And without Spence there, the reckless, wondrous feeling in her heart suddenly felt less like excitement than simply fear.

There were risks she'd never had the courage to take.

And with Spence, she was badly afraid that the cost of a mistake was the price of her heart.

Ten

There hadn't been a single call all afternoon, but the very instant Gwen immersed her hands squish-deep in meat loaf—predictable as rain—the telephone decided to ring.

Neither of the boys was likely to pick it up, assuming they even heard the ring. April had come over to play after school. After three solid days of rain, the kids were going squirrely from being cooped up. She'd kept them busy for a while making volcanoes out of laundry blueing and vinegar and construction paper—that mess was still cluttering her kitchen table— but she let them loose while she started dinner. They were chasing and yelling all over the house like a stampede of miniature elephants.

Rapidly she wiped one hand on a dishcloth and grabbed the receiver. She immediately recognized her youngest sister's voice.

"Have you talked to Abby?" Paige asked urgently.

"Not in several days. Why? What's wrong?"

"I don't know. That's the problem. I talked to her yesterday afternoon, and haven't been able to think about anything else ever since. Oh, Gwen, I think she was drinking."

"Drinking? Our Abby?" Gwen pressed the receiver tighter against her ear to hear over the banshee screams emanating from the Florida room. "Come on, she has to be practically force-fed a glass of sherry at Christmas."

"I'm telling you, she sounded sloshed."

"Well, maybe she was." Absently she sprinkled some pepper on the meat loaf. "You know how much stress Abby's been under with that huge promotion coming up. It's not like she committed some crime, if she took off for an afternoon and relaxed with a little wine."

"And that'd be fine. Except you know what a workaholic Abby is. She couldn't spell the word *relaxed* with a dictionary. She never plays hooky and she sure as patooties doesn't drink."

"I know, I know, but that's all the more reason—" Gwen started to say, then stopped. Her role, in any sisterly crisis, was to be the soothing voice of common sense.

Just then, though, her gaze accidentally strayed to the view outside her kitchen window. Nothing there but her rain-drenched patio. But her mind flashed to the memory of her birthday and Spence finding her on that patio after she'd been tippling in the cooking rum. Indulging in a few sips of rum had seemed pretty innocent, yet somehow it had turned into a catalyst for that first kiss from Spence. One kiss. That had exploded into an avalanche of emotion and events that still had Gwen feeling snowed under and reeling. "I'll call Abby," she said swiftly.

"Good. Maybe I'm imagining things, but I think she'll talk to you, if anyone. You've always had the most level head of all of us, kiddo."

Gwen squeezed her eyes closed, thinking *not anymore*. The conversation drifted to her sister's pregnancy, baby names, her brother-in-law's job, their parents' health. And then Paige predictably asked how she was.

Gwen almost told her about Spence, almost told her that she'd made love, was in love, that nothing in her life had ever been this wondrous, this incredibly heart opening, this special, this totally... terrifying. She didn't have to be sane for her sisters. She didn't have to make sense. They'd love and support her through thick and thin, no matter what she did. But somehow the words wouldn't come, even with Paige, and it felt selfish to even be thinking about herself when her oldest sister could actually be in trouble.

As quickly as she severed the call with Paige, she dialed Abby's work number in Los Angeles. A secretary informed her that Abby was out for the afternoon, so the best she could do was leave a message.

When she finally hung up the telephone, her mind was distracted, not at all on mixing meat loaf and making dinner again. She almost dipped her hands back in the mix, though, when she suddenly realized the house was quiet. Really quiet. Peacefully quiet.

Every maternal panic button instantly lit up on red alert. Grabbing a dish towel for her hands, she galloped to the doorway. Jacob, her ace-pro master at devilment and noise, was stretched out in front of an entire planetful of Lego in the Florida room. Any other time she'd have stood there and savored such a rare moment of her darling behaving like a saint...but April and Josh were nowhere in sight. Nor were they whooping and hollering.

This little stretch of peaceful serenity was wonderful. It just wasn't natural.

Hustling fast, she checked the bathrooms, then the living room, then hiked back toward the boys' bedrooms. She heard April's voice first, saying, "I don't want to do that. I think it sounds icky."

And then her philosophical Josh, responding matter-of-factly, "I know it sounds icky, but it's something you gotta do if you're in love. Donny Baker told me, and Donny knows everything about this stuff."

Then April, sounding wearily resigned. "Well, this better be all we have to do to get in love and have a baby, 'cause I don't like this part about swapping spit. I think it's gross city. You sure there isn't another way?"

When Gwen stepped into the bedroom, she found both children stark naked, rolling on the floor, and as far as she could tell, in the throes of experimenting with the joys of French kissing.

"Spence? Do you have a minute free? I know it's late, but I wanted to wait to call you until the kids were all asleep. A little, um, delicate problem came up that we need to talk about."

"Delicate problem?" Spence mentally braced. Once April had gone to bed, he'd switched on his laptop computer for a quiet hour of work, but now he quickly exited the program. For three days he'd been waiting for Gwen to be willing to talk to him. Really talk.

He heard her clear her throat. "I don't really want to bring it up over the phone. Let's just say the course of true love doesn't always run smooth."

He heard the humor in her voice; he also heard anxiety. A porcupine-sharp knot formed in his stomach. And twisted. But she went on swiftly, "I'm not trying to be suspenseful. This is just something better discussed face-to-face. The boys are dead to the world, but I don't want to leave them alone in the house for long. If it's okay, I'll just pop over to your place for a couple of minutes?"

"Sure, it's okay."

It didn't take three minutes for her to jog across the yard. Time enough for him to switch on the back porch light, be waiting at the door and build up a few more porcupine-sharp knots in his stomach.

She emerged from the shadows with a flushed face, her eyes darting straight to his, then just as swiftly away. She was either uneasy or embarrassed about something, which surprised him no more than her warning about a "delicate problem." Her scoopnecked top and wraparound denim skirt were pretty typical attire for a hard, mom-duty day, but the skirt flap teased with a show-off view of one bare long leg as she jogged in his back door.

He snagged her wrist, stole a kiss before she could get any words out. It wasn't outright piracy since she instinctively hooked an arm around his neck in response. He tasted rose lip gloss and nerves. Electric nerves. Desire shimmered between them like a velvet bolt of electricity, worse than before they'd made love. Much worse.

He'd had a lid on some patience before. Now he knew how incredible she was, how hot and wild Gwen could be when she let go. And so, judging from instinctive and yearning reaction, did she. Her eyes turned luminous, vulnerable. Her body tipped toward his like she was that tower in Pisa and he was her sole source of gravity. Her responsiveness triggered his arousal with the speed of a jack-in-the-box.

In the last three days she'd "accidentally" popped over for coffee once. He'd "accidentally" shown up for lunch. Neither had been hungry for the sustenance of lunch or coffee. He couldn't get enough of her, and Gwen...she hadn't shied from those encounters. By nature she was an earthy sensualist, and emotionally giving, but like a bud bursting open, she flowered lush and wild with a lover she trusted. But there'd been no time or chance to discuss that interesting quality of trust. Their few moments together had been stolen between work and children's schedules.

She lowered down from tiptoes after that kiss, her cheeks streaked with color and her mouth red—but she rolled her eyes at him. "Don't you start with me, McKenna. This time I really do need to talk with you."

"It was just a kiss," he defended teasingly, but his spirits were sinking lower than a well. He knew they couldn't keep doing it—hiding around, sneaking around. Even a few days of trying it had underlined how impossible an affair would be. A little forbidden excitement was fun, but Gwen was dead-serious responsible about her kids. And so, dammit, was he.

His heart thunked like the pendulum tick of the hall clock. She'd come to call it off, he thought. He knew damn well she was scared of the building relationship between them, scared that any relationship with a man meant being trapped again. The last thing he wanted to do was clip her wings, but to prove that, he needed time with her. Much more time.

And that kiss had diverted her attention. But not for long enough.

Temporarily, at least, her eyes sparkled with pure feminine devilry. "That was hardly just a kiss," she scolded. "It was an invitation to mayhem and you know it. You're an incredible amount of trouble, McKenna—"

Hell, he was sure trying to be.

"—but we have a problem. And I'm afraid it's touchy. An extremely delicate matter concerning love and sex."

That was exactly what he was afraid of.

"Josh and April are planning on eloping."

"Huh?" Spence heard her. It just took a second for his brain to make any synapse connection. He'd been so positive the sensitive problem Gwen had wanted to discuss was them, that the kids' names seemed to pop up from an alternative universe. "Beg your pardon?"

She nodded briskly. "I found them naked in the boys' bedroom. It seems there's a kid in the fifth grade who's offering free sex education to the younger set. They were, um, doing their damnedest to master the art of French kissing. This fifth-grader apparently told them if they swapped enough spit, they could make a baby."

"Josh? April? Naked? French-kissing?"

"Uh-huh. As they explained it to me, they're not only in love. They're engaged. I don't know if you noticed the trash bag tie April has on her finger, but that's, um, their engagement ring."

"My six-year-old is engaged?" Spence repeated. "I may need a minute to recover from this."

"*You* need a minute? I almost had a stroke when I found 'em naked. And I know, I know, kids play doctor. Curiosity's healthy. And natural. But holy cow."

"Holy cow doesn't begin to cover it. My daughter, my baby, my innocent angel, already tumbling into the clutches of an older man. I mean, Josh *is* a second-grader—"

"Don't you dare start laughing, McKenna," Gwen warned him darkly.

"I'm not, I'm not. But I definitely think we need a drink—something strong and potent to deal with this shock." He opened the fridge. "Milk or OJ?"

"OJ."

"Yeah, this is hardly a milk moment." He filched two glasses from the cupboard. "You first. Poor baby, you were the one stuck finding 'em and having to deal with it. What'd you do?"

Gwen crashed on the stool by his island counter and rested her weary chin in a palm. "I fumbled, pretty badly," she admitted morosely. "I made 'em put their clothes on. And I said that we respected each other's privacy, and that meant that boys and girls kept their private parts covered around each other."

"You call that fumbling? I call that brilliant fast thinking."

"Yeah, well, it didn't work worth beans," Gwen said. "Your daughter immediately piped up and said wasn't it different because they were in love? I'm telling you, this whole thing is gonna take some careful handling. I mean, they're both dead serious, Spence. They *are* in love. Puppy love. Which has to be one of the most painful, vulnerable experiences known to mankind.''

Spence took a reinforcing slug of OJ, his eyes on her face. Not that the children's problem wasn't serious, but he still felt like a death-row inmate with a reprieve. She hadn't come over to deliver a Dear John speech. His pulse was still thumping relief. "April was talking ten for a dozen about marriage at dinner tonight. But she talks ten for a dozen all the time. I didn't have any reason to think the marriage subject had any special context.''

"So far," Gwen said dryly, "they haven't planned too much beyond having a baby and their elopement. But before you leap to the conclusion that my son was leading her down the garden path, I have to tell you that your daughter had both hands on my son's, um, whatchamacallit.''

"It took two hands to handle that whopper? And he's just seven?''

"McKenna! Darn it, if you make me laugh, I'm gonna shoot you! This is serious. I think we should agree on how to handle our precocious monsters together.''

So did Spence. Personally, he thought a call should be made to the school to put the fifth-grader who was doling out the "free advice" out of business. Gwen concurred. As far as handling their two lovebirds, he was basically inclined to let the course of true love play itself out. "I think some extra supervision is called for. Or just watchfulness. I don't see letting them play naked, but I don't think raising a royal conniption about it is a good idea, either. Forbidding a kid something seems the surest way to arouse their interest even more.''

"Agreed on that, too," Gwen said, and then hesitated. "I really wasn't sure how you'd feel about this. I know some parents would have a major moralistic stroke."

"Well, I'd love to have a stroke. But I think kids at six and seven are just starting to get a concept of morality. They're old enough to have a sense of right and wrong, but when they come across something new, we're talking the power of curiosity. They don't automatically put a moral framework on everything."

"Yeah, I find the same. And I try and save the *absolutely forbid* words for issues involving safety. If you tell kids *no* before they're old enough to understand a *why*, you're missing a chance for them to learn and think things out on their own."

"So...are we gonna let them plan a wedding, tiger?"

"I'm thinking that we should be careful of their feelings, careful not to make fun of them. But maybe we can both try talking them into the benefits of a long engagement."

"Sounds like a plan to me. Uh, Gwen?"

"What?"

Spence scratched his chin. "Maybe we're gonna skate through okay on this one. But if they're this precocious at six and seven, I'm never gonna survive their teenage years."

Gwen laughed. "You think we should start buying Maalox by the carton now?" And then, "Oh, shoot..."

She'd just noticed the time. Spare seconds later, Spence stood in the doorway, watching her fly home across the yard, her hair catching beams from the moonlight. She didn't have the same monitor paging system he did, and even with the boys asleep, Gwen was Gwen. No way was she willing to leave them alone in the house for long.

He rolled his shoulders restlessly. He loved that woman. He'd fallen hard, deeply, completely. But every moment they shared made him feel like he was wading deeper and deeper into quicksand.

He'd loved watching her test her newfound feminine wiles on him. He'd loved watching her slowly gain confidence, trust in her own judgment and independence. And he'd sure as hell loved giving her that taste of wicked recklessness she hungered for.

No matter how potent the chemistry between them, though, it was moments like tonight that he wanted her to see. How well, how naturally and honestly they handled a touchy parenting problem together. How many values they had in common about kids and families and life. How easily they shared the struggle to be good parents—and, yeah, how they were able to laugh together at that struggle sometimes. They belonged together, he thought fiercely.

But *belonging* was a word Gwen had good reasons to be afraid of, and Spence felt trapped in a catch-22. To express his feelings was to risk Gwen feeling pressured, the same way her ex had push-and-pressured her. She needed the right, the time, to decide how she felt about him freely. Love was about freedom. Hers. His. Theirs.

But Spence also needed time to prove that to her and was damned scared the hourglass was running out. Maybe it hadn't happened tonight, but an affair was so unviable around the kids that Gwen was bound to either fish or cut bait before long.

* * *

Gwen waved goodbye to the boys as Ron's car pulled out of her drive. When they were out of sight, she spun around, thinking she had a whole quiet evening to get some work done. But her gaze latched onto the phone, and on impulse, she dialed next door. "Spence? You're going to think I'm a nut for calling, but I just had to tell you something quick—"

"The last time you 'just had to tell me something,' I nearly got an ulcer. April couldn't possibly be trying to seduce your son again. I just dropped her off at a sleep over, supervised, all girls, safe and sound."

Gwen chuckled. "No, this has nothing to do with sex and six-year-olds. Although the romance seems to be still going pretty hot and heavy. Josh loaned her his favorite Nintendo game."

"God, not that. It must be love. But if you're not calling because of another immediate crisis with our lovebirds..."

Gwen twisted the phone cord around her wrist. "No, nothing about them. It's just...well, Ron just picked up the boys for the weekend. He wasn't here two seconds before he started in with his usual nit-picking—Jacob didn't have the right shoes, Josh needed a haircut. And Spence...I started laughing."

"Laughing, huh?"

"Well, darn it, I know it sounds silly. But you're the only one who knows I started at the bottom of the class at Mouse School, coach. And I wasn't laughing to be mean, but honest to Pete, I could suddenly see how emotionally constipated he sounds sometimes. And that's all it took. A little laughter, a little relaxing, a little 'not buying in' to his criticism routine. I couldn't believe it. He quit being a pistol and he backed right down."

"Sounds to me like you just got an *A* in that assertiveness class, ma'am."

"Nah, this wasn't like Rome got conquered in this little confrontation, but it still felt so good I had to tell you. I stood up for *me*, McKenna. Imagine that. I just had to let you know those lessons of yours paid off."

Gwen squeezed her eyes closed, suddenly feeling foolish for having wasted his time with the call. There just seemed no one in her life who would understand this little "victory over wimpdom" but Spence. Still, she severed the call quickly.

Five minutes later, when he knocked on her back door, her jaw dropped in surprise—and must have dropped a whole foot farther when she saw what he was carrying. French champagne and Russian caviar.

"Spence, you nut! I didn't do anything to earn champagne and caviar! This is crazy!"

"Well, crazy's a relative term. Some say you'd have to be certifiable to like caviar... but I vaguely remember your mentioning that you'd always wanted to try it. And with all the kids gone for the night, this seemed like as good an excuse as any."

He asked her to find crackers, and while she scrounged in the cupboards, he battled with the champagne cork. It blew like a bullet, foam sizzling all over his hands, making them both chuckle. They moved to the living room, where he spread the cotton throw from her couch on the carpet like a picnic blanket.

She was in old sweats, hardly dressed for an elegant champagne minifeast, and as she knelt next to him, she kept telling herself *Keep it light. Keep it fun. Don't you dare make too much of this, Gwen Stanford.* Spence was a friend, a fellow single parent, a coach—and yeah, he was her lover, but she was doing her painful damnedest to keep that in perspective.

She was a cookie maker. With a past history of making a man her whole life. She never wanted to make that mistake again, and she'd never doubted that Spence's life was peppered with sophisticated, savvy women in business. Dynamos. Like him. Gwen knew the chemistry between them was real, knew he valued the friendship, but she'd have to be crazy to build up cockamamy romantic dreams of forever with him.

Being careful to keep things light and easy between them was the key, and that light mood worked wonderfully. For a time. Spence made a campy, dramatic production of spooning an exact moundful of beluga caviar on the cracker. "This is like the oysters," he instructed her. "You just can't try caviar in a sissy fashion. It takes guts. You gotta go for broke—the whole cracker in one shot."

"Hey, watch who you're calling a sissy there, buster. This isn't the old Mouse-Gwen you're talking to. I'm ready." She promptly popped the cracker in her mouth. And almost died. Swallowing fast, she grabbed the champagne glass and literally emptied it in chugging gulps. Then it took her a second to recover from a choking cough. "It's good, it's good. The taste just...surprised me. I wasn't expecting it to be so salty."

"Liked it, did you?" His eyes glinted pure devilment.

"Umm..."

"There's sure nothing on the planet that tastes quite like it. Extremely expensive. A rare indulgence. A treat like none other. You ready for more?"

"Umm..."

"Believe me, you can have it all," Spence said gravely. "Given a choice between road kill and caviar, I can't swear I'd vote for the road kill... but it'd be a close vote."

Startled, she let out a chuckle of relief. "You don't like it, either?"

"Can't stand the stuff."

"But it's so expensive. We can't just waste it."

Spence scratched his chin. "Well, we could bury it in the backyard and hope it has some use for fertilizer, but I think we'd be risking killing the grass. Maybe for several years."

She had to laugh. But later, even days later, she couldn't remember how or why that laughter and lightness had turned into a different mood entirely. There was just this sudden... silence. Cheerful lamplight glowed on all her familiar living room clutter, the rose-and-white sofa, the flowers spilling from the porcelain vase, the crafts and photos and plants crowding every surface. Yet all she saw were his eyes looking at her.

And then coming for her.

Dizziness roared in her ears before his mouth even claimed hers. There was no blaming the champagne for causing this brand of dizziness. It was strictly him. Her pulse suddenly charged like a fire was racing through her blood. He had a hand under her sweatshirt before she could think. She had a hand pushing up his T-shirt before he could.

She was so sure this urgency would have quit before now. They'd made love; the edge should be off that hunger. She couldn't need him. It frightened her to believe she could need Spence; she'd battled so hard to change and build in some gut-real strength and self-reliance. Yet it was like striking tinder to flint, every time they touched each other.

And getting worse. He anchored a leg between her thighs as he leveled her onto the cotton blanket. She could easily feel the swell of his erection, hard as marble but warmer, alive, pulsing. He wanted her to feel it. He wanted her, now, with a need and speed that made her heart spin. In the cramped carpet space, his elbow cracked against a coffee table leg, and her foot smacked against an easy chair. "This is beyond nuts," he growled, "we're going to kill ourselves in here."

But he didn't get up and move toward the bedroom, and neither did she. The instant she ruffled the T-shirt over his head, his mouth was aiming for hers again. She was waiting just as impatiently to kiss him back. As swiftly as he yanked off her white sweatshirt, his lips journeyed down her throat to her breast, sucking on her nipples until they tightened into raspberries and hurt, hurt so good, hurt with the sweet-hot fire of desire.

She tasted and nibbled and kneaded right back, wherever she could reach, pushing at his clothes until zippers and buttons and fabric finally gave. He kicked his pants off the rest of the way, making them both bare, which could have appeased this fierce desperate urgency and instead only seemed to incite more. Her fingers dug into his shoulders, clutching him, so that when he rolled she was straddling him on top. And Spence suddenly slowed down the forest fire.

"You want to do the riding this time, tiger?"

The night air washed over both of them, not cool. Nothing about her body or mood felt remotely cool, but she suddenly felt vulnerable and exposed. He gripped her bottom, positioning her so that she could already feel that hard ridge begging entrance into that dark, hollow emptiness inside her. His voice was as smoky as sex, husky with promises she knew intimately well he could keep. He knew her. But not this way. And old inhibitions suddenly reared their naked heads.

"I won't do it right," she blurted out.

"There's a way to do it wrong?" His eyebrows arched. "What a hell of an exciting thought. Do it wrong, tiger. There's a slim chance I might last more than two seconds, if you could manage to do it wrong for just a little while." His voice lowered to a rogue's whisper. "I want you too much. And too damn fast."

Spence just didn't understand that it took courage for her to take the initiative—something she'd always been genetically short on. She always worried about performance, feeling tested, not doing things right or well enough to please him. But the damn man started whispering, distracting her, daring her with that low wicked voice of his. She *meant* to worry. He just made it impossible to concentrate, and somehow it was easy, her moist warmth easing his entry, her muscles clamping around him so naturally.

"God. If this is what you call wrong, I want a sworn promise you never figure out any other way," he hissed.

"McKenna, you're impossibly easy to please."

"Maybe that's because you're impossibly easy to love."

She heard the fever in his voice. The fever of tenderness. And there went the last inhibition she owned. Her spine arched back, her body taking him, taking him, beginning a driving rhythm and ride that she could have sworn she didn't know. This galloping wonder of freedom she felt, deep on the inside, came from him, with him. Only with him. Blood sluiced through her veins, exultant, hot. She felt like she could have soared off a cliff. And then she did, in a friction-sharp plunge toward ecstasy, holding Spence so tight she could have sworn she touched his soul.

He more than touched hers. Love filled her heart, overflowed, spilled all through her. He had so changed her life. She knew what he meant to her. She knew what he'd brought her. And she told herself fiercely that it didn't matter if he loved her back.

At that moment she even believed it.

Eleven

Gwen had proposed the dinner together. Spence thought it'd be fun, but she knew better from the start. A masochistic love of torture had nothing to do with this. She needed a whomp upside the head—a whomp of reality—and on this earth, there couldn't be a more guaranteed way to self-deliver one than taking both families and all three children to McDonald's.

"Three Happy Meals, two Cokes, one Sprite, two Big Macs and a large fry... Gwen?" Spence turned to face her.

"A Big Mac and fries'll do for me, too. I'll get the napkins." She herded her rambunctious sons toward the condiment counter. The instant her head was turned, Josh elbowed Jacob, and Jacob naturally retaliated by slugging his brother. "Look, you guys. You can either settle down or go sit in the car, your choice."

"He started it," Josh said heatedly.

"I did not. You did. He called me a wiener and a bug-face, Mom," Jacob said plaintively.

"I'm not interested in who started it. I'm interested in seeing manners and good behavior when we're out in public—or you die. It's as simple as that. Now I mean it, you two. Chill out. *Now.*"

They subsided...for a few minutes. Spence appeared with the mounded tray of food—and his so perfectly behaved angel of a daughter. "Could I sit with Josh?" April asked the adults.

"Of course you can, honey," Gwen responded.

Of course, once the lovebirds took one side of the booth, Gwen was packed into the other side with Jacob between her and Spence. Squished sardines had more elbow room. Spence winked at her over the kids' heads. "Ah, the price we pay for love," he murmured under his breath.

"Why can't I sit with Josh and April?" Jacob demanded.

"Because the chances of your not slugging your brother, on a scale of one to ten, are about a hundred and fifty on the doubtful side. Ketchup, anyone?"

The first plastic tube of ketchup squirted in a spurt on the window. The culprit was unknown, but could have been any of the three. Then the kicking under the table began. Then came the effusive bubbling into the straws, accompanied by gross animal noises and show-off burping. Then came an out-of-control giggle attack, which was naturally more contagious than the flu.

Gwen rubbed a napkin on the window, took a bite of a Big Mac and watched for the first spill. There'd be one. She just didn't know when or how bad—yet.

The dinner was going exactly as she'd expected, she thought morosely. Well, *something* had to kick her head out of the clouds. She'd been dreaming about Spence. Not just at night, when she'd wake up with damp, twisted sheets. But when she was supposed to be working or carpooling or chaperoning a field trip to the St. Augustine Fort. She would dream they belonged together. She'd dream their love was so huge, so powerful and unique, that they could overcome all obstacles. She was in so deep that Spence seemed an inseverable part of her life, part of her air, as necessary to her as water.

He mattered so much that she was scared. Soul scared. He'd mentioned love, but the word and the emotion were easy to express when two lovers were naked together. Gwen never believed he meant it. They had something special, but if Spence's heart were inclined to be snared by a woman, she'd always pictured him with his natural mate—a sharp, cool, poised go-getter. She had, in fact, mentally pictured him with dozens of women. None of them were remotely related to a hard-core cookie maker.

There was nothing wrong with being a cookie maker. Over the course of their relationship, Gwen knew she'd changed, gained confidence and a sense of being true to herself that she'd never had before. But that was the point. Spence had become the best friend she'd ever had, someone she could be honest with about who she was. And she refused to lose that friendship because her emotions were way, way out of control.

Dinner together with their monsters was a fine, fine way of obliterating any romantic dreams from her mind. Not just for now. She didn't figure she was going to forget this lesson when she was 110.

"I don't know who's kicking," Spence said gently to the world at large, "but you don't want me to look under the table to find out."

All kicking ceased.

Jacob suddenly piped up, "I think we need an alligator, Mom."

"Oh?"

"Yup. There's places where they're dying. People just kill 'em to be mean. That's what we learned in school today. There's whole bunches of alligators that just got to be protected or they'll be murdered. I was thinking we could keep one in the bathtub."

"I think it's against the law to keep one in the bathtub, sweetheart." She took a napkin to his face. Jacob, being Jacob, considered eating to be a whole-body experience.

"Are you *sure* it's against the law?"

"Well, not dead sure," Gwen admitted, "but pretty sure. And I think an alligator would feel awfully lonely, all by itself in a bathtub."

"I have an answer for that."

"You always do, lovebug."

"We could get two. Then they wouldn't be lonely. And we could protect two from being murdered." He shifted his eyes to Spence. "Could you talk my mom into it?"

"I'd walk on water for you if I could, sport, but I'm afraid you're on your own with this one. I can't talk your mom into anything."

"I have that trouble, too. But my teacher says we have to *care*. And I care, Mom."

"And I'm so proud of you for caring..." From the corner of her eye, she caught a Coke tipping. Spence had the same parental instinctive reflex. He grabbed it before she could. Their eyes met.

"Did you know the S'minole Indian guys could have a coupla wives, Mom? But they quit that a while ago. My teacher says it's 'cause they got some morality. Also because having two wives was too much trouble."

"My, you learned a whole bunch of things in school today, didn't you?" She couldn't seem to stop looking at his eyes. Awareness lasered between them. The kids, the noise, the smell of Big Macs and fries, the messes...reality was right there, loud enough to slam some common sense into even a demented woman. But...

"Yeah, the S'minoles are really cool. They drink this really yucky stuff called a Black Drink. And the kids don't have to go to school if they don't want to. And they live in the 'Glades, where there's lots of alligators. *Their* moms probably let them have all the alligators they want."

"You think so?" Maybe she was demented, Gwen thought helplessly. It felt like she was touching him. The air between them seemed like an invisible silk-paved road where only they could travel, only they could communicate. Sexual vibrations hummed between their eyes like a love song. Only it was more than sex. It was a plumb-crazy feeling that she'd never stop hearing that love song, not with him, and it didn't make a lick of difference where they were or what they were doing.

"Yikes!"

Startled, Gwen's head immediately swiveled toward the sound of the enraged yelp coming from Josh. Spence spun around, too, just in time to see April squish a plastic container of ketchup on Josh's head.

"*April!*" Spence thundered.

"He called me a sissy, Dad," April said, and then to Josh, "You call me a sissy again, I'm gonna punch you good."

"You *are* a sissy." Josh pushed both hands into his hair, effectively spreading the mess and managing to coat his hands with ketchup at the same time. Then he aimed his dripping, red palms for April's face. She shrieked loud enough to wake the dead.

Spence whipped out of his seat and had the two separated in seconds. "You're not punching anyone, April, and you're never pulling that ketchup thing on anyone again, either. You owe a big apology to Josh. Now."

"But, Dad . . ." Gigantic crystal tears brimmed.

"I said *now.*"

So much for the tears. "I'm sorry about the stupid ketchup," she snarled.

Spence wasn't through. "Josh, apologize for calling April names."

Her son's chin jutted out. "Hey, you're not my dad or my mom—"

"If you think that gets you off the hook, I've got big news. Teasing is one thing, and calling someone names to hurt their feelings is another—and you know the difference. Don't waste your time looking at your mom, because I'm the one talking to you. Apologize. Now."

"I'm sorry," Josh snarled.

"The men," Spence informed Gwen, "are now going into the little boys' room to see what cleanup miracles we can pull off."

"Yeah, let's go scrub Josh up." Jacob bounded from his seat. "Ho-boy, ho-boy, this is mens' work, huh, Spence? 'Bye, Mom."

The girls were left alone, Gwen bemused at how fast and effectively Spence had handled World War III. His daughter, though, had cupped a pouting chin in her hands, and those big blue eyes were spitting upset tears. "I hate men," she announced. "And I'll bet you're really mad at me for getting ketchup all over Josh."

"Well, I think there are better ways to handle getting mad. Especially in public, lovebug." Gwen reached over with a napkin so the little one could blow her nose. She *meant* to look stern. Spence had managed to. Spence had done the just-right discipline thing. But somehow all she could think of was how much she'd come to love his blond, blue-eyed angel with the irrepressible devil streak.

"I thought Josh loved me forever," April said sadly.

"Sometimes men are just the pits," Gwen agreed.

"Well, I'm gonna forget boys for the rest of my life." The pipsqueak soprano reeked of wisdom. "It just isn't worth it."

Josh echoed those sentiments when she tucked him in several hours later. "*You're* okay, Mom. But otherwise I'm gonna forget girls for the rest of my life. The other ones are nothing but trouble."

She kissed his cheek and smoothed back his cowlick. "Maybe you want to leave just a little door open.

It's possible you might change your mind in a few years."

"Spence was mad at me," he mentioned.

"Mostly, I think he was mad at April. But you earned your share. Are you square with him now?"

"Yeah. He's okay."

That *okay* echoed in her mind as she wandered into the Florida room. All three kids had naturally accepted Spence's brand of discipline. All three, in fact, had behaved as if they were part of a family—give or take that April and Josh didn't plan to speak for the rest of their lives.

Considering the catastrophe the dinner had turned into, everyone was okay. Except for her. Her pulse was chugging, her heart thumping with anxiety.

She cleared the toys off the coffee table, switched on lamps and spread out papers. After weeks of researching, she'd accumulated a mountain of information on what it took to become a day-care provider. The laws and licensing. First aid. Facility requirements. Which psychology and child development courses were particularly geared for someone interested in the field.

Unable to concentrate, she jumped up twice and headed for the phone, but both times stopped herself. She'd already talked with both her sisters this week. She was concerned about Abby. As her younger sister had already guessed, Abby sounded tense and high-strung and anxious, not like herself. Threatened with the ultimate weapon—that her sisters would show up to help—Abby would undoubtedly choose the wise option and eventually spill whatever was really wrong. Until then, Gwen could not see badgering her further.

Still, she normally needed no excuse to pick up a phone and call her sisters. No matter how different they all were, Paige and Abby loved her. They might pry; they might bicker and argue, but Gwen knew she could count on them for support in any time of trouble. And God knew, she was in trouble.

Vaguely she heard a distant sound, but it barely penetrated her thick, murky mood. She sat on the couch, staring blindly at the papers in front of her, feeling . . . lost.

She'd grown up so sure of the rules. If she was just a good girl, a good wife, a good woman, she couldn't make a mistake. Ron had been part of that picture-perfect dream. Everyone in her universe had told her how lucky she was to "land him," a good looker from a good family, a doctor, a charmer. A girl couldn't make a mistake if she had the good sense to choose a prize catch like Ron.

Only she understood now, that she'd sold herself a lie. Being good had never protected her from making mistakes. The sure, safe women's roles had never been safe at all. And months ago, breaking out had seemed like a reasonable answer. Not because she really wanted to indulge in reckless, selfish behavior, but because, tarnation, she needed to explore and test whatever the real Gwen Stanford was made of.

"Hi, tiger."

There, in the doorway, was the source of her pulse-chugging anxiety. Typically, damn him, Spence looked like her personal dream of a lover, the Sean Connery eyes, the roguish grin that obliterated her sanity, the lean elegance that made every witless female hormone sit up and say "Hi there."

"I didn't hear you come in," she said.

"I can see you're pretty deep in thought. I brought the pager over in case April wakes up, but she's really sleeping hard. Thought I'd come over to make sure you survived dinner."

That was exactly the problem, Gwen thought darkly. She hadn't. Dinner should have been guaranteed "safe." No one enduring a meal at McDonald's with three small children could conceivably be distracted by romantic, loving, desirous thoughts. Only she had. And this restless, frightened, anxious mood had been hounding her ever since. For him, though, she managed a smile. "Put three kids that age together with food, and only a hard-core idealist could expect to digest anything peaceably."

"It could have been worse. Offhand, though, damned if I know how." She saw his wry grin. He moved closer, from light to shadows to inside her light again. His gaze drifted to the papers blanketing her coffee table. "You look really busy. What's all this?"

When he stepped closer, her first instinct was to scoop all the papers out of his sight. But she stopped herself.

This was it, she thought. There wasn't going to be a better time to put a lid on her Pandora's box of fantasy dreams. Somehow she'd been playing with his life and feelings. With her own. That had never been her intention, but Spence's gaze rested so warmly, so intimately on her face. If somehow the new clothes, the new hairstyle, the reckless lover she'd tried to be had swayed him into believing she was a different woman from the real Gwen Stanford, it was more than past time to own up and be honest.

"Spence," she said quietly, "I need to tell you something."

* * *

Spence saw her sudden stillness, had noticed her white-faced edginess the instant he walked in. "So tell," he encouraged, and dropped down on the couch next to her.

"I've made up my mind about changing careers."

"Yeah? That's great." Because her eyes kept nervously darting to the jumble of files and figures on the coffee table, his did, too. "'Licensing for Day-Care Center Regulations,'" he read aloud from one. "So that's what you're looking into?"

She nodded, her chin tilted just an eensy bit toward the bulldog stubborn side. "I love kids. Always have. I could financially manage going back to school, and I looked at all kinds of careers. But all the high-powered jobs, the fancy careers, the real money-makers ... Spence, they're just not me."

Her love or affinity for children was hardly headline news. Spence couldn't fathom what he'd walked into, what had her upset. There was fear in her eyes, anxiety, that he couldn't place for love or money. "The last I knew, the reason you were looking so hard at a career change was to make damn sure you got into something you loved this time."

"Yeah, exactly. And when it came to the wire ... I just can't make ambition or some kind of career with clout important to me. I'm a mom. A cookie maker. I just plain love caretaking little ones. I think I'm going to be stuck being a nurturer-type when I'm ninety."

He watched her rub her arms as if she were suddenly cold and, not for the first time, felt like he was wading through quicksand. Her nervousness was contagious. "Tiger, everything you've said sounds great. Running a day-care center would seem to be right up your alley. So how come you're looking like something's really wrong?''

"Nothing's wrong. To me, the whole thing is exciting. I just..." She swallowed, hard, as if a thick lump of cotton was jammed in her throat. "Spence, I was afraid it would sound boring to you. Ordinary. The thing is...I can't do it, McKenna. Turn myself into a dynamo. Peanut butter always did turn me on more than diamonds. You've been such an incredible coach. And you've helped me with so much. And I didn't want to think I'd let you down by—''

"By standing up for the rights of peanut butter over diamonds?''

On the tail end of a shaky breath, she said, "I don't know where you thought we were going together. But if anyone helped me see how important it is to be honest with myself, it's you. And the real, naked truth is that I'm gonna be peanut-butter ordinary until I die, McKenna.''

Before she could inhale another shaky breath, he hauled her into his arms. Roughly, not gently...to match a hot, rough, hard kiss that wouldn't wait a second longer to express.

She hadn't let an insecurity sneak out, like a weed poking through grass, in a while now. She'd been mastering the art of standing up for herself damn well, particularly considering what a long hill she'd had to climb from the critical, confidence-eroding el-jerko she'd been married to. That she'd pinned down work she loved and wanted to pursue gave Spence joy. That she hadn't needed or depended on anyone's support to follow through with it gave him more joy.

His lover was getting downright feisty.

But that she thought he was more attracted to diamonds than peanut butter was a misconception that required immediate correcting. And he could have sworn he'd been extremely clear before on his definition of exciting. Maybe not clear enough.

So he gave her a liquid kiss. And then another one.

Her arms slid around his neck. Her lips parted under his, her response wild and willing, fervent. Free. It was always this way. He touched her, and she opened her generous heart and took him in, the way no woman had ever touched him, ever wanted him.

Frustration speared, then snapped inside him like a coil stretched too taut. Her drumming heart thudded against his own; her quickening breath echoed his; her supple body molded perfectly against him. They were a matched set. She *had* to see it. And while the fever was rising fast, already tempting both of them to lose control, he raised his head.

"Tell me what you feel," he said.

It slipped out like a forbidden whisper, hopelessly loose in the wind. "I love you, Spence."

"Do you?"

"Yes."

"Then tell me what you want, tiger. Shout it. Tell me."

Her eyes widened. His sudden harsh tone had obviously startled her. Her hands slipped, then dropped from his shoulders. She searched his eyes . . . but she said nothing.

Despair lanced through him. In business, in life, it was so easy for him to take charge. With Gwen, he'd always known that was the wrong way. If he pushed her, if he made her feel pressured, she could always

believe that he was cut from the same cloth as her ex.
She wouldn't feel free. Unless she was.

But what she wanted had to come from her. Or they
had nothing.

And from her continued silence, that sure as hell
seemed to be what she was telling him.

He pushed off the couch and aimed for the door.

Twelve

"Jacob, Josh. I'm just going to carry this pie over to the McKennas'. I won't be gone longer than five minutes—but you two be good."

Her two angels delivered a cross-your-heart promise without a qualm. Gwen was less than reassured. Holding the fresh honey pecan pie with hot pads, she used an elbow to crook open the back door. She could hardly gallop across the yard carrying a hot pie, but hustling was wise. She loved her darlings. She just didn't trust them alone together for longer than two shakes of a lamb's tail.

She didn't trust her courage would hold out for too long, either.

Spence, she knew, was upset with her. Last night, she had never anticipated the conversation to suddenly turn into a vulnerable confrontation about love and their future together. When he'd stalked out of the house so fast, he had clearly been hurt—seriously, painfully hurt—at her failure to respond.

Some might consider the honey pecan pie to be a peace offering. Heaven knew, her first instinct with a man used to be the old traditional woman's role of accommodation. Whenever her ex was miffed, she would rush right in to please and placate.

She'd definitely changed, Gwen thought darkly. Her first instinct with Spence was to give him a whomp upside the head. She'd been *trying* to answer him last night. But the words had all been tangled in her throat—he'd turned her on, for Pete's sake—so it was his own damned fault if her mind had been on desire and him. *His* doing, not hers, that she hadn't been coherently logical.

So the pie wasn't a peace offering. It was just... a foot in the door to reopen communication. A swift one, because she had to get to the boys. But her heart had felt gripped in a tight fist all day, knowing she'd hurt him, and she just couldn't wait all the hours until the kids were asleep before doing *something*.

At his back door she yoohooed a greeting. When no one answered, she juggled the pie, pushed at the door latch and poked her head in. "Hello? Mary Margaret? April? Spence?"

So close to the dinner hour, she expected to see pots bubbling on the stove, Mary Margaret bustling around, lights and noise—but there was nothing. The table wasn't even set. "Spence?"

His car was in the driveway, so she knew he was home from work and around somewhere. For a millisecond she considered dropping the pie on the counter and sprinting back home. The thought of running was tempting—as tempting as putting heroin in front of a recovering addict. Running away from confrontations had always been one of her best skills. Still, it seemed that she'd broken that old, handy habit, too.

She put down the pie for a few seconds. But only long enough to push a hand through her hair, straighten her coral print skirt, and briefly clutch the cameo at her throat for luck. Maybe her heart was thumping with a coward's fear, but she swallowed hard and moved on.

"Spence? April?" Finally, a few steps into the hall, she heard voices emanating from the living room. One of them was an adult female voice—Mary Margaret's, she assumed, and smiled at the image of the housekeeper's reaction to the dessert. Mary Margaret had a sweet tooth that could compete with any of the kids'.

But it wasn't Mary Margaret she found with Spence. Gwen charged through the living room doorway too quickly to apply the brakes. The wreath of a smile on her face froze. The cheerful hello she intended to deliver jammed in the back of her throat.

The woman in Spence's arms was tall and svelte. As fast as a camera flash, Gwen took in the swath of mahogany hair, the dramatic makeup, the emerald suit and navy pumps. The woman wasn't gorgeous, just put together. Perfectly. A model of taste and sophistication and expert styling. Exactly—*exactly*—like the kind of woman Gwen had always pictured with Spence.

The hurt was so sudden. Like a bullet had slammed a hole in her soul, stinging sharp, fast and bitter. She couldn't seem to breathe. Spence very obviously had his arms around the woman voluntarily. He was hugging her. Tightly. Warmly. Thoroughly.

He also quickly realized she was standing there, because his head shot up. One hand dropped from the brunette, but certainly not with the speed of the guilty. "Hi, tiger."

He called her tiger? Right in front of the other woman? Words tumbled out of her mouth faster than a babbling stream. "Geezle beezle, I'm so sorry to barge in. I couldn't rouse anyone when I yelled from the back door. Really, I'm sorry to interrupt. I just happened to be baking this afternoon and I brought you over a dessert...." She exhibited the pie, feeling like a fool, but hurling the thing at a wall didn't seem like a politically correct option. Disappearing was the only driving thought in her head, and she rapidly back-stepped toward the door.

"I can smell the pie from here—thanks, Gwen, does it ever look fantastic. I'll even get the first chunk, because Mary Margaret took April for the evening to a party with her grandkids. And somehow I'm neglecting introductions here. Gwen, this is June Roberts. And June, this is..."

Temporarily there was nothing in her brain but Jell-O. She heard the name, heard the words of introduction, but it took all her mental and emotional energy to concentrate on smiling—and not looking at Spence. She definitely couldn't face looking at Spence right then. "I'm out of here," she said cheerfully. "I'll put the pie on the kitchen counter. And that's all I came over for, to deliver the pie—"

"Gwen, wait a second—"

"No, no, I left the boys alone. And dinner cooking. I'll see you later, and real nice to meet you..." Gwen was going to tag on the woman's name but she'd already forgotten it.

As she tore out of the house, she couldn't swear to remembering her own. She raced across the yard faster than a track star, barreling into her own kitchen with lungs working overtime and her heart slamming, slamming. Slamming like fire.

"Josh? Jacob?"

Contrary to maternal expectations, the boys hadn't killed themselves in her brief absence—but they were starved. She threw together some macaroni and cheese, mopped a spilled glass of milk, fixed a broken toy, hurled dishes in the dishwasher, drew the boys' baths. Josh had some new questions about God and wanted to know how toothpaste was made. Jacob wanted to show her some magic tricks. Then came the bedtime rituals.

She'd have let the children stay up. Maybe forever. But for the first time in mom history, neither son gave her a lick of grief over going to bed and were snoozing hard before nine. The house was abruptly as silent as a nightmare...except for the painful, insistent beating of her defenseless heart.

She headed for her bedroom, intending to kick off her shoes and strip down. Instead, the light glinting off the bureau mirror snagged her attention.

The cameo at her throat glowed in that soft light. As she reached up to unlatch the pendant, her fingers hesitated midair. She'd worn the cameo as a talisman for luck. Right now, heaven knew, she felt as lucky as the survivor of a train wreck.

Still, she hesitated, suddenly remembering her thirtieth birthday and her first reaction when she saw the cameo. The profile of the woman in shadow had reached her right where it hurt. The symbol had been so strong, of how long she'd lived in Ron's shadow, and her birthday had been the crossroads when she'd come to face it.

Funny.

But the way her heart ached, it seemed like now, tonight, this moment, was the real crossroads. For weeks now, months, she'd really known it wasn't Ron—or any other man—who'd chased her into the shadows. It was her. Allowing her insecurities to rule her life.

No one ever stopped her from standing up for what she wanted.

No one ever stopped her from shouting what she needed.

The woman staring back at her in the mirror certainly had no resemblance to that stunning brunette she'd found in Spence's arms. But it wasn't the old Gwen in that mirror, either. There was pride in the tilt to her jaw, strength in that brow, depth in those dark brown eyes. Her aching heart changed beats, slowly, like an engine revving slowly on a winter day, building up momentum, building up speed to a full-blown rocket charge.

She'd never loved Ron this way. Never felt reckless and special and gutsily good about herself on the inside with any other man but Spence. Always she'd doubted that he could possibly feel the same. Always she'd been afraid of misjudging what their relationship meant to Spence.

But she knew damn well what he meant to her.

Spence was alone, on the kitchen phone, when she stormed in. No knock. She just sort of burst through that screen door the instant she spotted him, her hair wind tossed, her eyes full of lightning...and in bare feet, he noticed.

Later he realized that he'd hung up on a client midsentence. Not fast enough, apparently, because a coral-tipped fingernail was abruptly wagging in his face.

"I'm not in competition with anyone else. Not gorgeous brunettes, not blondes. Not anyone, McKenna, so you'd better get that through your head right now."

As a conversational opener, it lacked something in the way of a relaxed "Hello, how are you." But then Spence was braced for a tornado the instant he saw those flashing dark eyes. Very carefully, very gently, he said, "I couldn't agree more. It'd be a total waste of time for anyone to bother competing with you."

He'd tried that same calm, soothing tone with her that afternoon. It hadn't worked then or now. She wasn't listening. She was too busy pacing and wagging that finger. "There is no possible way to pursue an affair with three small children around, for Pete's sake."

"Yeah, I agree."

"Dammit, Spence. It's time to fish or cut bait."

"Yeah, I agree."

"I want you to listen and hear me out."

"Okay."

"You already know me. The bad and the good. I'm a mom, a homebody, a chronic cookie maker. A woman struggling not to be such a stupid softie all the time—but I'm a long way from the doormat I used to be. And I happen to love you, McKenna. With all my heart. For the record, it's a tough, strong woman's heart, so this isn't mouse bait I'm offering you—"

"Tiger—"

"No, don't you tiger me. I need to finish saying this. She isn't for you, buster—"

He wasn't positive that she intended to let him get a word in, but shouting was a new experience for Gwen. Temporarily she ran out of breath, and he took his chance. "If for any reason you're referring to June…she's May's sister, Gwen. April's aunt. It seems that she and her husband just moved. She used to live on the East Coast, and she came to see me to ask if it was all right if she took an active part in April's life. She got emotional, started crying. That's why I put my arms around her. That's the only reason. She was upset."

That stopped Gwen dead in her tracks. "April's aunt?" she echoed.

"Yes. She was estranged from May for years. They barely talked. But she felt bad that she'd neglected to build any kind of relationship with her only niece." He added carefully, "And I know you—if you'd have been here, you'd have hugged her exactly the same way."

"Well, yeah, I probably would have." She shifted on her feet. "You never had to explain about her," she informed him.

"No?"

"No. Just because I had a jealousy attack the size of Kansas doesn't mean that I don't trust you, McKenna."

"You do. Trust me," he repeated.

"For heaven's sake, you're adorable," she said impatiently. "Unless the entire female population suddenly turns blind and doddering, women are obviously going to throw themselves at you from time to time. I'm not saying I'm thrilled at the idea, but I'd hardly be stupid enough to get involved—much less fall in love—with a man I didn't trust. Completely. And another thing—"

"Hell, tiger, I can hardly wait to hear 'another thing.'" The poker of tension rammed up his spine was slowly, slowly relaxing. He hadn't been sure if it was okay to breathe since she walked in the room. He'd never seen her so wired for sound before.

Or so scared. She stopped her frenetic pacing for a second and met his gaze. A dread of rejection was as clear and naked as pain in her soft brown eyes. Yet she still laid more vulnerable honesty on the line. "I would never try to hold you with a noose around your neck, Spence. Maybe I'm talking about rings, but I'm not talking about one through your nose. For a long time, I thought Ron's controlling possessiveness meant he loved me. That's not love, McKenna. At least not the kind of love I feel for you... or want with you."

He took a step forward. Then another. Her hands had been fidgeting almost nonstop, pointing a finger, or propped on her hips or wrapping around her arms to hug herself. Now, while she was suddenly standing totally still, he could see all the defensive actions for what they were. Her fingers were trembling. And cold. Ice cold, at least until he captured them in his own.

Her face tilted up to his. All those guts she didn't think she had blazed in the fire in her eyes. "I'm good for you, coach," she whispered.

"Believe me, I know you are."

"It was hard for me to see that I had something to offer you. Something...equal. But maybe if I'd never been such a dependent mouse type, I'd never have understood what real freedom was. I stumbled on every rock in that road, and I know what I want now. A life partner. Someone I love and trust. Someone who isn't threatened by my growing in my own directions. I've always felt free with you, McKenna. It just took me a while to realize that the freedom to feel, to be myself, to grow, was what two lovers could bring each other. And that's exactly the kind of love I would give you back."

"I was scared you'd never see it. Afraid you'd never feel it." The need to hold her wouldn't wait. Even another second. He gathered her up, swung her arms around his neck and sealed her mouth with a kiss. He had never been sure it would happen. Her shouting at him. Her shouting for them. A hundred emotions spilled into that kiss: hunger and joy, pride in the woman he had been so lucky to find and even luckier to love, all the promises for the future he could suddenly taste. "I love you, Gwen."

"And I love you right back." There still seemed to be a smoking storm in her eyes, but fear definitely wasn't fueling it. He caught the hint of a dangerous smile—a wicked, reckless woman's smile. And not that he was paying all that much attention to geography, but she seemed to have taken his hand and was leading him right to the master bedroom. "Honestly, McKenna. I'm supposed to be the wimp half in this pair. And you left it up to me to do the proposing?"

"Not by choice. It damned near killed me not to ask you months ago." Hell, *she* made him kiss her again. "You were never a wimp, Gwen, but I didn't know how to make you believe it. I was afraid to tell you what I felt, afraid you'd feel pressured, that you'd think I was a steamroller type like your ex. I never wanted to push you into corners, tiger. I just wanted to make things possible for you."

"I'll show you exactly what you made possible," she warned him. There were shadows in his bedroom, but then she switched on the light. All the shadows disappeared.

His lover was definitely in the mood. She was beyond beautiful, although Spence suspected it could well take a lifetime to really show her all the beauty he saw, all the strength and fire in her impossibly generous heart. It was the kind of work a man dreamed of. And she was the only woman he ever wanted to share that dream.

Hours later she pulled the covers up on the bed and snuggled next to him. "Spence?"

"Hmm?"

"You *are* a steamroller. You pushed me right off an emotional cliff. Mercilessly. Ruthlessly. Thanks."

"Umm, Gwen?"

"Hmm?"

"You steamrollered me right back. Pushed me right off that same emotional cliff. Scared me out of my mind. Thanks."

"You ain't seen nothing yet," she murmured. And Gwen, being the pure female dynamo she was, proceeded to take charge and show him.

*   *   *   *   *

Abby's story is coming soon!
Watch for THE 200% WIFE—Jennifer
Greene's first Special Edition novel, coming
July 1997. It's a THAT SPECIAL WOMAN!
you won't want to miss.

In February, Silhouette Books is proud
to present the sweeping, sensual new novel
by bestselling author

CAIT LONDON

about her unforgettable family—*The Tallchiefs*.

TALLCHIEF FOR KEEPS

Everyone in Amen Flats, Wyoming, was talking about
Elspeth Tallchief. How she wasn't a thirty-three-year-old
virgin, after all. How she'd been keeping herself warm at
night all these years with a couple of secrets. And now one
of those secrets had walked right into town, sending
everyone into a frenzy. But Elspeth knew he'd come for
the *other* secret....

"Cait London is an irresistible storyteller..."
                                              —*Romantic Times*

Don't miss TALLCHIEF FOR KEEPS by Cait London, available
at your favorite retail outlet in February from

Silhouette®

Look us up on-line at: http://www.romance.net   CLST

Take 4 bestselling love stories FREE

Plus get a FREE surprise gift!

Special Limited-time Offer

Mail to Silhouette Reader Service™

3010 Walden Avenue
P.O. Box 1867
Buffalo, N.Y. 14240-1867

YES! Please send me 4 free Silhouette Desire® novels and my free surprise gift. Then send me 6 brand-new novels every month, which I will receive months before they appear in bookstores. Bill me at the low price of $2.90 each plus 25¢ delivery and applicable sales tax, if any.* That's the complete price and a savings of over 10% off the cover prices—quite a bargain! I understand that accepting the books and gift places me under no obligation ever to buy any books. I can always return a shipment and cancel at any time. Even if I never buy another book from Silhouette, the 4 free books and the surprise gift are mine to keep forever.

225 BPA A3UU

Name	(PLEASE PRINT)	
Address	Apt. No.	
City	State	Zip

This offer is limited to one order per household and not valid to present Silhouette Desire® subscribers. *Terms and prices are subject to change without notice.
Sales tax applicable in N.Y.

UDES-696   ©1990 Harlequin Enterprises Limited

Harlequin and Silhouette celebrate
Black History Month with seven terrific titles,
featuring the all-new *Fever Rising*
by Maggie Ferguson
(Harlequin Intrigue #408) and
A Family Wedding by Angela Benson
(Silhouette Special Edition #1085)!

Also available are:
Looks Are Deceiving by Maggie Ferguson
Crime of Passion by Maggie Ferguson
Adam and Eva by Sandra Kitt
Unforgivable by Joyce McGill
Blood Sympathy by Reginald Hill

On sale in January at your favorite
Harlequin and Silhouette retail outlet.

Look us up on-line at: http://www.romance.net   BHM297

Beginning next month from

▼ SILHOUETTE®

Desire

by
**Elizabeth
Bevarly**

Watch as three siblings separated in childhood
are reunited and find love along the way!

ROXY AND THE RICH MAN (D #1053, February 1997)—
Wealthy businessman Spencer Melbourne finds love with the
sexy female detective he hires to find his long-lost twin.

LUCY AND THE LONER (D #1063, April 1997)—
Independent Lucy Dolan shows her gratitude to the fire
fighter who comes to her rescue—by becoming his slave
for a month.

And coming your way in July 1997—
THE FAMILY McCORMICK continues with the wonderful
story of the oldest McCormick sibling. Don't miss any of
these delightful stories. Only from Silhouette Desire.

Look us up on-line at: http://www.romance.net   FM

SILHOUETTE® Desire®

COMING NEXT MONTH

#1051 TEXAS MOON—Joan Elliott Pickart
Family Men
Private investigator Tux Bishop, February's *Man of the Month*, was determined to help feisty Nancy Shatner and keep her safe from the danger that threatened her. But who was going to protect her from him?

#1052 A BRIDE FOR ABEL GREENE—Cindy Gerard
Northern Lights Brides
In a moment of loneliness, recluse Abel Greene advertised for a mail-order bride. But when spunky wife-to-be Mackenzie Kincaid arrived, would the hesitant groom get over his prewedding jitters?

#1053 ROXY AND THE RICH MAN—Elizabeth Bevarly
The Family McCormick
Wealthy businessman Spencer Melbourne hired P.I. Roxy Matheny to find his long-lost twin. But the last thing he expected was to lose his heart to this spirited beauty!

#1054 LOVERS ONLY—Christine Pacheco
Clay Landon set about winning back his soon-to-be-ex-wife Catherine—no matter the cost. But would a seduction at a secluded hideaway lead to a passionate reconciliation?

#1055 LOVECHILD—Metsy Hingle
Jacques Gaston was a charming ladies' man who couldn't commit. But when he discovered beautiful Liza O'Malley had given birth to his secret baby, could Jacques find it in his heart to become a loving father and husband?

#1056 CITY GIRLS NEED NOT APPLY—Rita Rainville
25th book
Single father Mac Ryder didn't want delicate city-girl Kat Wainwright on his land. He knew that she wasn't prepared to deal with the dangers of Wyoming, but that wouldn't keep the rugged rancher from teaching greenhorn Kat about love.

Eau Claire District Library

Eau Claire District Library

You're About to
Become a
Privileged
Woman

**Reap the rewards of fabulous free gifts and
benefits with proofs-of-purchase from
Silhouette and Harlequin books**

Pages & Privileges™

**It's our way of thanking you for
buying our books at your
favorite retail stores.**

**PROOF OF
PURCHASE**

SD-PP21

Offer expires March 31, 1997

**Harlequin and Silhouette—
the most privileged readers in the world!**

**For more information about Harlequin and
Silhouette's PAGES & PRIVILEGES program call the
Pages & Privileges Benefits Desk: 1-503-794-2499**

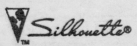

Silhouette®

SD-PP21